Deadly Pack

DEADLY PACK

Deadly Trilogy Book 3

Ashley Stoyanoff

Ashley Stoyanoff Books
London, Ontario

Also by Ashley Stoyanoff

CHEATING DEATH SERIES
Going Rogue
Secrets and Lies

DEADLY TRILOGY
Deadly Crush
Deadly Mates
Deadly Pack

PRG INVESTIGATIONS SERIES
Two Truths and a Lie
Play It Again

THE SOUL'S MARK SERIES
The Soul's Mark: FOUND
Waking Dreams, A Soul's Mark Novella
The Soul's Mark: HUNTED
The Soul's Mark: BROKEN
The Soul's Mark: CHANGED

OTHER TITLES
If I Could Do It Again
Jingle Bells and Witchy Spells
Halloween in Hell

Dedication

For Hazel, because you kept me sane.

CHAPTER 1

AIDAN

A ghost of a smile touched Jade's lips as I reached over and squeezed her hand. Wispy strands of hair framed her face, pieces that had worked their way loose from the twisted knot that was piled high on her head. Her scent was cluttered with emotions, the dense, sour-sweet aroma of sorrow being the most prominent.

Her gaze was calm, though, as it slid around our clustered circle, stopping for a beat on each face before moving on to the next. She held onto my hand with a loose, dry grip and nodded her agreement as plans were made and strategies were formed. She hadn't really said much of anything since the pack had left, and I didn't know what to think of that. Jade wasn't really the quiet type, and, dammit, her silent agreement to everything was unnerving. It made me think she had her own plans brewing inside that beautiful head of hers.

We were standing in the clearing, hashing out the last few details of what needed to be done. Dominic paced a few feet away, his phone glued to his ear, arranging Jared's cremation. Jade had been adamant about that. *"Jared's claustrophobic,"* she'd said. *"He wouldn't want to be buried, trapped underground, inside a small box. We'll spread his ashes here. He loved this place."* It had been the only words she'd uttered in the last twenty minutes that had held any trace of emotion; every other mumble that came from her lips had been blank and toneless.

Across from where we were gathered, Jared's body was being loaded into the back of Tommy's pickup truck. I didn't miss the fact that Jade was trying hard not to look, and I also didn't miss the way her throat worked hard when she caught sight of Tommy from the corner of her eye as he lifted the lifeless wolf form and carefully placed it onto a blanket in the back of the truck. Her nose was screwed up, wrinkling along the bridge, and her eyelashes fluttered quickly as she tried to fight against the fresh spring of tears that glossed her eyes.

Her inner turmoil was unbearable to watch. And it completely sucked that I didn't know what to do to make this easier for her.

Her gaze followed Tommy as he began folding the edges of the blanket over, cocooning Jared within it. A painful, gasping sound fell from the back of her throat as the blanket was draped over Jared's face, and in a beat, she swiveled, turning into me, and buried her face into my chest. Her hands fisted my shirt, and she held on to me as if I were her lifeline.

And my heart cracked, splintered, broke, as my strong, independent mate started to fall apart.

The guys fell silent as I wrapped my arms around her waist, giving her a moment to pull it together. I felt her body quake against me. She was breathing deeply but raggedly, her shoulders lifting and falling, and she pressed her face further into my chest.

I rested my chin on her shoulder, brushing my lips against her ear. "It's okay, sweetheart," I murmured.

"It's okay." The words felt impersonal, and they sounded like a lie. I really didn't know if it would be okay. I didn't know if she'd be able to get past this, but I did know that I would do everything I could to make this easier for her. "Tell me what you need from me, and I'll do it. Anything. Tell me how to help you deal with this."

Jade didn't answer for a long moment, so long that I really didn't think she was going to, but then she whispered, "I'm okay, Aidan." Her voice was thick and raw, and her breath hitched on a hiccup. I felt her throat constrict and bob against my chest as she swallowed, and then she said, "I'm good. Promise. I'm just overwhelmed and a little ... um ... scared?"

"Are you asking me or telling me?" I asked, stroking my hand up and down her spine as I held her close, trying to soothe her. She sounded so lost, nothing like the fierce, feisty, bullheaded girl that I knew.

She craned her neck back and looked up at me. For a second, I saw her pain and anger blazing in her eyes, but it didn't last. She blinked a few times, smoothed out her expression, and pasted on a cool, fake smile. "I'm scared," she said with certainty.

My heart squeezed tight as if someone had wrapped it in an elastic band. Scared wasn't good. Fear could turn the best-laid plans into a disaster. A disaster that the pack (and the town) seriously didn't need right now. I squeezed her tightly and muttered, "Fear is only excitement in need of an attitude adjustment."

Chris chuckled, and my gaze snapped up to his. His eyes were dancing with humor, most likely remembering the first time my dad had said those words to me. He'd been there, so had Tommy, standing beside my father. I'd been just a kid, and I'd been terrified when they'd decided it was time for me to learn what an alpha's scent could do. Those words had been my dad's version of a pep talk, and I seriously couldn't believe that I was actually using them now.

Jade huffed and wiggled out of my arms. Her lips thinned, and she attempted (and failed) to give me a fierce scowl. She placed a hand on her hip, her bottom lip still trembling. "Are you saying I need an attitude adjustment?" she asked, quirking an eyebrow in question.

I nodded, grinning down at her. "Yep."

The guys stood motionless, watching Jade warily as if they were all waiting for her to flip out on me. The truth? I kind of was, too. Actually, I wasn't just waiting for it. I was hoping she would. I needed to see something other than the gut-twisting pain that marred her pretty face, and anger would have been better. It would give her something else to focus on, something other than fear.

But Jade didn't flip out. Instead, her lips stopped trembling. The corners of her mouth quirked up a little, and the elastic band that had been squeezing my chest snapped at the sight of her small smile.

The silence lingered for a long moment, but as Jade's smile grew, Marcy broke it and asked, "Is that a smile?" She inched closer to us and tried (unsuccessfully) to stifle a nervous giggle.

"No," Jade said, shaking her head and turning around to scan the group. "Definitely not a smile."

"It looked like a smile," Mark said. He was smiling, too, but it didn't come close to reaching his eyes. He had the hood of his sweater down; his crazy mop of curls was flipping all over the place in an unruly mess. He held Jade's eyes for a moment. His softened a little, and his pained smile tugged up a bit further.

Jade groaned and looked away quickly to hide the new flood of tears that pooled in her eyes, I assumed, and she said, "This is not the time for smiles, guys. We need to focus here."

"There's always time for smiles," Mark countered. "Life would be pretty damn depressing without them."

And I thought Mark was right. No matter how bad it got, making time for laughter and smiles definitely helped.

I knew the smiles I saw curving the team's lips were for Jade's benefit. They were trying hard to make her okay, to show her they were okay. And even if they weren't directed at me, those smiles, although small and pained, made it pretty damn clear that they weren't holding Jared's death against me. Well, at least that was how my brain decided to read them, and I found myself seriously hoping that my brain was right.

"It's all set," Dominic said, and he thumbed his phone as he made his way back to the cluster surrounding Jade and me. "They'll do the cremation today, and we can pick up his remains tomorrow."

There it was. The last piece we'd been waiting for before moving out.

The smiles faded, blurred, died, replaced by solemn expressions, and a determined vibe spread through the air. The hardness returned to the enforcers' gazes. We knew where the bastards were now. There was no more waiting. No more excuses.

"Time to move," I said, taking Jade's hand and giving it a little squeeze. "Landon, Beck, Craig, and Mark, you guys are with Tommy and Chris. Get as close as you can, but not close enough that they'll pick up your scent. You're just confirming what Jeff told us, nothing else. Seventeen cougars and no women. That's it. Then come straight back and report. Got it?"

I waited for the nods, watching them closely to make sure that they got it, but they didn't nod. Nope. Lips thinned, anger spiked in the air. And I found myself thinking — again — that sending them out was probably not the best plan. Not only did they just watch their brother die, but each one of them had been helping Jared screw me over in one way or another while he tried to get revenge for their father — another family member of theirs that was dead because of me.

I was about to voice my thoughts, tell them I'd find another group to go, when Jade said, "Guys, I know you're ready to take them out, but seriously, you're just confirming the location. Tell me you've got this because I cannot focus on what I have to do if I'm worried about you guys."

Their silence held for a second longer before Beck nodded. "We've got it." His steely eyes focused on me, and he said, "I can see your doubt, Aidan. It's over. Let it go."

I held his gaze for a beat, searching for any hint of malice behind his guarded expression. He held firm, so did the others, and even though I wasn't sure I believed him, I couldn't pick up any trace of a lie. I nodded stiffly and pushed on. "Erika, you're with Dom. Take Jared and keep your phones on. Mac and Trevor, head back to the headquarters and work on something for when his remains are picked up. Plan for tomorrow night. Jade and I will take Richard's body to her dad." I looked down at Jade, squeezing her hand again, and asked, "Everyone clear on what you need to do?"

A round of *yeses* spilled from the group, and then everyone started moving.

Dominic hopped into Tommy's truck with Erika, starting it up, and with a quick nod in my direction, he eased out of the clearing. Trevor grunted a goodbye as he snagged Marcy's hand, towing her to his car. The guys started to shift, Tommy and Chris with them. It didn't take long before they were trotting off into the trees.

And as they disappeared, Jade started to shake again, and small sob-like whimpers escaped her lips.

"Hey," I said, dropping her hand and then tapping her chin up to meet my eyes. I brushed a thumb along her cheek to catch the stray tear that had managed to leak out. "Don't worry, sweetheart." I framed her face within my palms and kissed her chastely. "They'll be back soon," I said against her lips.

And they would. They were simply going to confirm that the cougars were at the newest location. Try to confirm Jeff's count of seventeen. Make sure we weren't going to walk the pack into a death trap when we attacked.

She blew out a noisy breath from her nose and whispered, "This morning, the happiness ... it feels like a lifetime ago." Her bottom lip started quivering, and she quickly tugged it between her teeth.

Damn, she really was breaking. I frowned. I felt it, the shift of my lips, the bunching skin along my brow, and I was sure my eyes didn't conceal the knot of panic that clogged my throat. The most perfect thing in my life was breaking, and I didn't have a clue how to fix it.

When I left my parents and my old pack, I never thought I'd have my own pack, let alone have someone like her in my life. Someone precious. Someone to protect. Someone to love.

But Jade Shaw had quickly become the center of my world. And I was supposed to protect her, keep her from being hurt, but since we'd met, all I'd managed to give her was pain.

And I knew this was just the beginning. How would I put her back together when this was over, when her father was dead? Just thinking about it made my chest feel all knotted up.

I cupped her cheeks in my palms, caressing them as

I stared into her big brown eyes, wishing for her smile, even a small trace of it, to come back.

Jade scrunched her nose up and pulled out of my loose grip. Her lips thinned, and she craned her neck back, cutting me a dirty look. "Don't look at me like that," she snapped.

"Like what?" I reached out, tucking a stray chunk of hair behind her ear.

She moved back a couple steps, out of my reach, popping her right hip out and planting a firm hand on it. Her face smoothed, her gaze turned serious, and she said, "Like you're worried I'm going to break."

I folded my arms across my chest and scanned her from tip to toe. "Are you?" My tone was casual as if I were just curious, but really, I was kind of freaked out that she just might break before this was over.

She shook her head slowly, deliberately. "No." Her voice was strong, certain. It was just too bad her tone didn't match the unstable and unsure spike in her scent.

CHAPTER 2

JADE

"You don't have to come with me," Aidan said.

I swiveled in my seat, looking over at him. I knew I was gaping, and I figured I looked completely stunned, but I couldn't help it. That was pretty much the last thing I'd expected him to say. His words should have sounded like a thoughtful gesture as if he were just looking out for me, but they didn't. His tone ... his scent ... well, if I had to guess, Aidan didn't want me to go with him.

But the thing was I had to go. There really wasn't a choice here. The man was my father, my flesh and blood. I had to be there. I had to do this.

"I'm not going home," I said. "I've got to do this."

Aidan dropped one of his hands from the steering wheel and squeezed my knee gently, reassuringly. He stole a small glimpse at me and smiled, just a tiny upward twitch at the corners of his mouth, before returning his gaze to the road.

And it confused me. Like really, really confused me. The gesture was supportive, just like his words were meant to be, but that scent ...

I figured he probably thought I'd interfere, try to

delay things, and give my dad a fighting chance, and I didn't know how I felt about that. Hadn't I just proven that I'd stand behind his decisions? I didn't interfere with Jared, at least not a lot, and I wouldn't with my dad. My dad didn't deserve my interference.

And even if I wanted to delay things, it wouldn't — couldn't — happen. Except, I knew with everything in me that if I asked for more time, Aidan would grant it in a heartbeat. And knowing that freaked me out. A part of me, a small, scared part, wanted more time almost desperately, and it made no sense. Dad didn't deserve time. His pack didn't deserve time. Still, something inside me wanted that time. But I knew, *I knew,* I couldn't ask for it. I wouldn't let my pack down. Not this time. Never again.

Aidan's hand was still on my knee, his thumb rubbing a gentle back and forth sweep on the inside of my leg. I glanced back at him, noticing his tight jaw and the white-knuckled grip of his other hand on the steering wheel.

"I'm serious, Jade," he said. "I can take you home." He looked sideways at me, another little smile, then back to the road. "You could start getting things ready for tomorrow. Help Mac with the planning."

Tomorrow. I wasn't really sure how Dominic had pulled that off so quickly. I knew Marcy's dad, one of the detectives in Dog Mountain, had a hand in it, but still, Jared's cremation seemed ... rushed. But then, I guessed rushed was probably a good thing right now. It wasn't as if we had days to plan, and really, Jared would have wanted something simple and quick.

I wiggled in my seat, fidgeting with the seatbelt strap that ran across my chest. "I'm going with you, Aidan." My throat felt dry and prickly and sore, and I swallowed hard, trying to clear the sensation. "I need to see him. I need to do this."

Aidan's response was a frustrated growl. I glanced over at him hesitantly, watching his jaw tick and his fist clench tighter on the steering wheel. He didn't look at me this time, not even a little glance. His thumb stopped moving on my thigh, and his scent ... changed. I breathed in deep, trying to place the new aroma. It was thick, tangy. It was ... worry? Apprehension, maybe? I wasn't entirely sure.

"Talk to me," I said, reaching over and squeezing his thigh. Right then, I seriously wished I could read his mind because not knowing what he was thinking was knotting me up like crazy. "What's got you so freaked out?"

Aidan relaxed slightly under my touch. He sighed. "It's pretty clear you've hit your limit for today," he said. "I just think it might be best if I handle this one alone."

My inner-wolf squirmed uneasily in my belly, and I shifted in my seat, turning to face him fully. "Are you mad at me? Is that why you're trying to send me home?"

"No, sweetheart." He shook his head. "No, not at you. I'm mad at this whole screwed-up mess we're in," he said, with a ripple of irritation gliding through his tone. He let out another long sigh. "But not at you. Never at you." His eyes met mine, serious but somehow warm. "I just don't want you to break on me. If you need time to get it together, then I'm going to make sure you have that time."

"I'm good," I said. A warm flood of relief washed over me, and I laughed a little. He was worried about me, not about what he thought I'd do when we got to my dad's. "I really am. And I have to do this, even if it kills me. I have to. I'm not going to let them down. Not again. I won't." I paused for a second, watching his jaw clench, and that warm feeling of relief started to fade. "There's something else, isn't there?"

"Later," he said, gently but firmly. "Let's talk about it later, okay?"

I opened my mouth, and just as quickly, I closed it because I really had no idea what to say to that. He was right. I'd hit my limit hours ago around the time that Tommy and Chris had shown up at our house with the guys and shared what Jared had been up to. I'd surpassed my limit when Aidan shifted in the house, ready to kill them. And by the time we'd confronted Jared, well, I'd been way past the point of keeping it together. But somehow, I'd managed. The truth? I really didn't know how much more I could take before I lost it completely.

So instead of pushing it, I leaned into him, kissed his cheek, and murmured, "Okay, later."

Moments later, Aidan turned onto my old street, pulled past my parents' driveway, and then backed in. He yanked up the parking brake and put the car in neutral, but he didn't turn it off. He looked at me, his face blank, and said, "Let me handle this."

I nodded once to appease him, but the burning glint that flared in his eyes told me he knew I didn't plan on sitting back and keeping my mouth shut. He let out a frustrated growl and dragged a hand through his hair.

"Aidan," I said a little hastily as he cut the engine and pulled the keys from the ignition. "He's my dad. I know how to talk to him." I let out a long stalling breath, and then I lied, "And I'm okay. Honestly. I'm good."

Aidan didn't believe me, not for a second. But really, I knew he wouldn't. He turned into me, cupping my cheeks in his hands. "I've got this." His voice was rough and full of some emotion that I couldn't place, or more accurately, it was one that I didn't really want to place. He brushed his thumb along my cheekbone, his eyes searching mine. "You trust me, right? As your mate, I need you to trust me enough to know that I've got this."

And with that, he dipped forward, touching his lips to my forehead, and then before I could reply, he popped the door open and got out. He didn't waste any time as he made his way up the steps of my parents' front porch and pounded on the door.

I'd like to say that I followed him immediately. That my head was in the game and I was totally prepared for everything. I wished I could say that I knew he had this. But I couldn't do any of that. Nope. Instead, what I did was sit in the car, watching out the back window, blinking at his back, stunned and more than a little confused.

The front door opened. My dad filled the doorway. He smiled at Aidan, and it looked so warm and sincere. Dad even clapped him on the shoulder in greeting. And still, I held my breath, and I didn't move.

I watched the arm gestures as they spoke, and I watched Dad's smile fade a little. And then his eyes roamed over the car, and they locked onto me. He furrowed his brow and cocked his head, and I heard him call, "Jade?"

His voice snapped me out of my stunned moment. I pushed the door open and hopped out of the car in a flustered rush. I was so flustered and rushed that my foot caught on the door well, and I tripped. My heart jumped into my throat as I lurched forward, coming close to doing a face plant on the driveway, but luckily, the door was there to catch my fall. I steadied myself and called, "Yeah, coming," as I let the car door slam.

I took in a few deep breaths, attempted to school my expression, and then, although my brain tried to fight me, urging me to run away, I turned and started toward the house.

"Pumpkin, what's wrong?" Dad asked, stepping out of the doorway, past Aidan. "You're looking a little pale." He looked good in jeans and a beige knit sweater, like an average working citizen. The clothes. The smile. The warm, concerned tone he used with me as if he actually cared. Lies. They were all lies.

I met his eyes, and I thought about making something up for a moment, but really what was the point anymore? So instead, I said, "I helped kill Jared."

Aidan cut me a warning look, which I completely ignored as I padded up the steps. I brushed my hand along his back as I went past him and took a seat on the porch swing. The old chains creaked as I pulled my feet up underneath me.

"Jared," Dad said, and his eyes widened just a little. He glanced at Aidan, then back to me. "Jared's dead?" And all his warmth was suddenly gone. He looked suspicious and a touch excited, and seeing it made my stomach roll.

"Yeah," I said, glad I'd sat down because I really wasn't feeling all that steady anymore. "He wanted to challenge Aidan for alpha. He ended up attacking me and I kind of held him down while Aidan ..." I broke off as my stomach rolled again.

"Jared wanted to challenge for alpha," Dad stated as if he didn't believe it. He narrowed his eyes, glancing between the two of us. His nostrils flared as he took in a few noisy breaths, and he chuckled, grinning at Aidan. "You claimed her."

I clamped my mouth shut, mainly to keep my jaw from dropping. A look passed between my dad and Aidan. I wasn't exactly sure what it meant, but it meant something. *Something* for sure. Whatever it was, it effectively ended any further discussion of Jared's death or the fact that I'd helped make him dead.

"No, she claimed me," Aidan corrected, cementing my theory that the *something* explained Jared's motives for challenging for alpha. He moved over to me, planting a hand on my shoulder, and squeezed, a firm reminder to me that he had this. He waited for a beat, most likely making sure I got the hint, and then said, "Richard's body is in the trunk. He's one of yours. You can deal with him."

Dad's eyes shifted toward the car, then back to Aidan. "The point of giving him to you was so he could help you." His tone was impassive as if Richard's death meant nothing to him one way or the other, and I assumed that was probably true. "He's not much use to you dead."

Aidan shrugged. "Wasn't much use to me alive, either." It came out on a growl, and his hand clamped, pinching tight on my shoulder.

Oh, yeah, my mate totally had this. I gritted my teeth and pressed my lips together, keeping my mouth shut, but I was pretty sure that the look I cut him told him exactly what I thought because he loosened up on my shoulder a little.

"You came here to get me to clean up your mess?" Dad asked, his voice carrying a bitter, dark undertone, and his distaste showed clearly on his face.

Aidan raised a brow and gave Dad a look that said, *oh yeah*, but he didn't say anything. I figured that probably wasn't what Dad wanted because his eye started twitching, and he clenched and unclenched his jaw as he glared at us. He was losing control over his calm persona. I could see it. The lines on his forehead deepened, his eyes hardened.

Dad looked back at the car and then glared back at

Aidan, and it was at that moment that I decided I'd had enough. This conversation needed to end. Now.

"Dad," I said, drawing his attention. "Just deal with him." I looked up at Aidan. "And will you stop being a dick? He's been helping us. He doesn't have to, but he has."

A small, forced smile played at Aidan's lips. "I don't like it when someone hurts what's mine," he said. He reached out, brushing a thumb across my bottom lip, an intimate gesture, one that made me blush. "And he hurt you."

"Are we still on that?" Dad groaned. "You were going to make her leave. I helped you achieve that a hell of a lot more peacefully than you would have by dragging her out."

"Stop it," I said, hoping for annoyance, but it came out sounding a little too sweet. I totally blamed Aidan's lip touch for that. I stood up, shrugging off Aidan's hand, squared my shoulder, and met my dad straight on. I sucked in a few breaths, hoping to bury my unease, and spat, "We're close to finding them, no thanks to your little gift. You could save us some time and tell me where they are."

"I don't know their exact location, pumpkin." His voice was soft, careful, and so was his gaze. "They don't tell me until I'm called out. They think I'll slip up."

"I think that's bullshit," I said, and I was surprised that my voice came out calm and controlled because I felt far, far from calm. "I think you know. What I don't know is why you're trying to protect those monsters."

Dad jerked back a step as if my words were a physical slap, and at the same time, Aidan said, "Jade, that's enough." His tone was soft but packed full of command.

I chose to ignore him. So did my dad.

"I'm not protecting them," said Dad cautiously, raising a hand in surrender. "I'm trying to protect my family, and keeping them away from town keeps you and your mother safe."

"Safe!" My blood pressure rose, my heart pounding within my chest. "You call this safe? You pushed me into the middle of a war. You've made it my responsibility to act."

He laughed once, a startling sound. "You're the alpha female. You won't be fighting."

His assumption didn't improve my mood. My eyes flared, my fists clenched, and my entire body started to vibrate with anger.

"Hell, yes I will," I said with a fevered pitch. "Do you really think I'd send my pack out and not be there with them? What kind of a leader does that? We can't ask them to fight and then hide away until it's over."

I barely had time to suck in a breath before my feet were torn from the ground. Warm hands circled my waist, twisting my body around, and then I was dangling over Aidan's shoulder. I let out a gasping shriek and started to squirm as one of his hands gripped onto my butt, holding me firmly in place, and the other went to my thigh.

"Put me down, Aidan," I growled, smacking his back and kicking out because, really, kicking and hitting was the only rational thing to do while hanging over someone's shoulder.

Aidan chuckled and squeezed my right butt cheek. "Not a chance, sweetheart." And then he started moving, with me hanging over his shoulder.

"Wait a minute," Dad called. I heard the smile in his voice. "Jesus, Aidan, put my daughter down."

But Aidan didn't wait, and he didn't put me down.

He went straight for the car. He yanked the passenger side door open, dropped me in, and shut the door without a word. He turned his back to me and growled, "Get the body out of my car." And a second later, the trunk opened. The car bobbed a little as Richard was removed.

I blinked, stunned, staring at the window. Aidan stepped away from the door, moving toward the back of the car, and I reached for the handle, ready to follow him because, well, throwing me over his shoulder and tossing me in the car was seriously not cool, and I wasn't finished with my dad. Not even close. I grasped the handle and was about to pop the door open when I heard my dad's voice, and I froze.

"Aidan, we need to talk," he said. He sounded as though he were trying to hide his laughter, but there was a seriousness to his tone, too, and I swore there was an edge of desperation. "All of us. Your mating changes everything. There's more going on here than you think."

Aidan laughed. "Oh, yeah?" he said. "I thought you didn't know anything. Isn't that what you just told your daughter?"

"I said that I don't know where they are, not that I don't know what they want."

"I don't care what they want," Aidan said, and I was astonished by just how cold his voice was. "I won't negotiate with anyone that keeps women in cages and uses them like toys."

"It doesn't have to be like that," Dad said, and yes, he did sound desperate. So desperate that I swore I could almost smell it. Almost. And Jesus, had he just admitted that the cougars kept their women in cages? I felt shaken to the core. My chest seized up, and it hurt to pull in a breath. I swiveled around, trying to get a look at them, but the trunk was still open, blocking them from my view.

"No, it doesn't," Aidan said, and his voice had

gotten impossibly colder. "You better figure out what team you're playing for, Jeff, and quick. We'll kill them when we find them, and if you're with them, we'll kill you, too." And then the trunk slammed, and the door opened, and Aidan was in the driver's seat.

He gave me a quick once over before he stuck the keys into the ignition, but he didn't say a word. He was pissed. I knew it, I felt it, but I was pretty sure it wasn't directed at me.

"What was that about?" I asked almost cautiously, *almost* being the keyword, because the truth was, I was kind of pissed off myself and more than a little shaken.

Aidan started up the car. "It's probably nothing," he said. "Just more of his games."

"You threw me over your shoulder." My voice was a hissed whisper, and I cut him a dirty look as my face flamed with heat.

"I told you to let me handle it," Aidan said. He sounded amused. He looked it, too. He dropped the emergency brake, shifted into first, feathered the gas, and pulled out of the driveway.

I huffed and buckled up. "You knew I wasn't going to let you."

"Yeah," he said cheerfully, giving me that crooked grin of his. "I knew."

I didn't respond to that. I figured it was best not to engage in this conversation while my blood was still boiling over.

CHAPTER 3

JADE

Aidan was still grinning when he dropped me off at the pack headquarters, and I had to admit, his grin was contagious. By the time he'd pulled up in front of the building, the majority of my anger had dissolved into pesky annoyance, although I wasn't about to tell him that. No, I wouldn't tell him because if I did, I might then have to tell him that he'd been right. I should have let him handle things with my dad. And telling him, that would have led to an even cockier grin that would have made me feel like even more of a failure than I already did.

The whole idea of bringing Richard to my dad was to make him uneasy, and hopefully, that would cause him to slip up somewhere. It was not to let him know, or give him even the slightest hint, that we were on to him.

But, of course, I let my emotions get the better of me. Damn, I might as well have told my dad that we knew everything. I'd clearly let him know that I didn't believe a word he said.

Yeah, I really should have listened to my mate and kept my mouth shut.

Since Aidan left, I'd been telling time by phone calls. They were becoming predictable. Every five minutes, my father would call. I hadn't answered one of his calls, and I had no plans to do it anytime soon.

I sat outside on a picnic table, shivering, with my phone clutched in my hands. The wind was brutal, cold, and blowing hard enough to rock me as it came barreling through the trees. Branches creaked, and the tops of the pines bowed under its furious attack. The sky was filling up with dirty, dark gray clouds and the air smelled of crisp, fall rain, damp and cold and fresh.

Each time my phone rang, I silenced it. After the fifth call, I'd given up on looking at the caller display. I didn't want to know what Dad had to say. Okay, that wasn't really true. I wanted to know. The issue was I was a little freaked out that he was calling to tell me that the team had been caught.

Okay, so that was probably a ridiculous worry. Dad had been trying to convince Aidan to stick around. He'd wanted to talk to us. He'd even hinted that the cougars actually wanted something from us. He was probably reaching out to me because Aidan had shot him down, but still, I was worried nonetheless.

I pulled my arms around me, hugging myself tightly in an attempt to stay semi-warm. How had my day turned sour so quickly? Just this morning, I'd woken up as the official mate of the alpha male of my pack. We'd been smiling — happy — planning to spend a lazy day in bed.

And then life happened.

It was really the only way I could think about what took place this morning. *Life happened.* Because within the pack, Jared dying for his crimes was life happening, and if I let myself think about it any other way, I was pretty sure I'd fall apart.

"Where's Aidan?" a hard voice asked from behind me, cutting through my thoughts.

I glanced over my shoulder. Luken. He'd healed up nicely from his run-in with Jared this morning, not even a scratch left. He looked annoyed and slightly hesitant as he closed the distance between us. "Dom needed him for something," I said with a sigh.

"You're shivering," he said, stopping in front of me. His arms folded over his chest, his biceps curling up thick with the movement. "Come inside. Mac's been looking for you."

"I'm not shivering," I said, my teeth clattering as I said it. I decided not to acknowledge that anyone was looking for me because, honestly, I wasn't ready to deal with anyone (especially Marcy). She'd want to talk about my feelings. She'd want me to let it out. And that was exactly why I was sitting outside freezing my butt off.

My phone rang again, chirping and vibrating in my palm, and I quickly silenced it.

Luken narrowed his eyes, looking down at my phone and then back up at me. After a couple of beats of silence, he said, "That better not be your mate you hung up on."

"Really?" I hissed, and he narrowed his eyes further. I gritted my teeth, giving him a pointed glare. "It's my dad."

Luken looked at me awkwardly for a moment as if he realized just how much of a jerk he was being. He let out a muffled sigh and unfolded his arms, taking a seat beside me. His eyes warmed, although not by much. "You should've answered it."

"He should be calling Aidan," I countered, which was a ridiculous thing to say, and by the look I got, Luken thought so, too. I was just as much an alpha as

Aidan was, and the man (unfortunately) was my father. Of course, he'd call me.

I glared at him a bit harder, seriously wishing he would vanish. My glare didn't faze him. He made himself comfortable, propping his feet up on the bench. He had a pair of boots on, the edge of his jeans stuck at the top of his boot on one side. He unzipped his hoodie and shrugged it off, wrapping it around my shoulders, before leaning forward, resting his bare forearms on his knees.

"You should've answered it," he said again, but softer this time, almost caring.

I glanced back down at my phone and muttered, "Dad hasn't called me since he kicked me out." I met his eyes and whispered, "What if the guys got caught?"

"They weren't caught," he said. He sounded completely confident in that. "They're smarter than that. They'll be back soon, Jade."

I hoped he was right, but that ounce of hope didn't come close to chasing away all my doubts. My shoulders slumped, and I puffed out a slow breath.

"And then what?" I muttered as another shiver chased down my back. "We rush out on a mindless killing spree? I have my father killed? What if they're not all bad? What if they're just doing the only thing they were taught to do? It's not like they've ever lived among the human population like our pack."

Another gust of wind pushed at me, blowing loose strands of hair in my face. I shoved it back, tucking it behind my ears, and huffed. "I just can't figure out the *why*. Why were they raised like this? Why are only the men changed? Why was there a deal with our pack in the first place? I just don't understand. I don't get it."

My face felt hot — burning hot. I looked at Luken and cringed when I caught the hardness in his eyes. *Way to go, Jade,* I thought bitterly. *God, did I really just blurt all that out to him?* I should have swallowed it. It wasn't as if Luken and I were friends. Our one real conversation had been seriously tense, and he'd made it damn clear he didn't respect me or even acknowledge me as an alpha of this pack.

Luken must have noticed my unease. His expression softened and warmed further, and he said, "There isn't always an answer to the *whys*, Jade. Sometimes people do shitty things just because they can."

My phone started ringing again, and I went to silence it, but he snagged it from me before I could. He thumbed the screen and brought it to his ear. "Jade's phone, you've got Luken," he said and paused. "She's behind closed doors with her mate." He paused, listening. "Don't know." Another pause. "Tonight." His brow furrowed. "You'll have to take that up with her mate. Yep, I'll let him know. Later."

He lowered my phone and thumbed the screen. His brow pulled in, and he looked at me. There was a question burning in his eyes, one that I didn't think he wanted to voice and one that I was sure I didn't want to be asked.

The silence held between us as we searched each other's faces, and after a moment, I broke it, whispering, "Do I want to know?" I tugged my bottom lip between my teeth, trying to stop it from trembling.

He hesitated for a second and then said, "How about I give Aidan a call, fill him in, and let him decide." He said it cautiously as if he weren't sure what to do. When I didn't answer, he said, "Go on inside, Jade," making the decision for me.

And for probably the first time since I joined the pack (and maybe the first time ever), I did exactly what I was told without uttering a single syllable.

CHAPTER 4

AIDAN

Dominic was distracted, but then I guessed I was, too.

He was leaning against my car, watching Erika from the corner of his eye while he attempted to lecture me about the team. He talked in broken sentences, or maybe I was only listening to bits and pieces. Really, it could have been either at this point. But the parts I heard, I agreed on. I needed to pick a new head enforcer.

Erika was propped against the wall outside the funeral home, giving us space. Her eyes were glued to her cell phone as her fingers flew across the keypad. Dominic had been watching her since I pulled up as if he thought she'd run if he took his eyes off of her. I was pretty sure I should have asked what was up with that, but honestly, right then, I didn't really care.

I didn't have a good feeling. Not about the cougars, or about Jade, or the team. It all felt ... not right, leaving my gut pitted and twisted up in knots.

The sky was darkening quickly. Off in the distance, I could pick out the soft claps of thunder as a storm approached. The wind had picked up, carrying a damp chill with it, and I pulled my jacket closed, zipping it up.

Dominic paused in his half-hearted lecture, glancing up at the sky, and said, "It looks like rain."

"Yeah, it does," I agreed and let out a slow breath. I glanced at him; his features were blank, hidden behind his normally cool and collected mask. I knew he was trying damn hard to hide it, but I could still smell his worry in the air. I thought he was probably worried about the same shit I was. His thoughts never seemed to stray far from his best friend — my girl.

I let out a long breath and muttered, "She's breaking, Dom, and if she breaks, we won't stand a chance. The pack will feel it. They'll get nervous. They'll feed off her pain, her fear." I scrubbed at my face and raked a hand through my hair. "Damn, I already feel like I've been cut open like I'm bleeding from her pain."

"Dude, cut the drama. Jade's fine," he said distractedly. "She just needs some time in her head to work out how to feel about everything. I don't get it, but she loved Jared in her own way, and the same goes for her dad. What you're seeing is the normal Jade grieving process."

I felt even less good once he said that. In fact, I felt kind of sick. If anyone knew what she was feeling, it would have been Dominic. He knew her. Knew everything about her. I'd been hoping he would deny my worries, not confirm that she was hurting. And if he was right, and Jade was really grieving, it was because I'd taken someone from her, and it seriously sucked that I was going to take even more.

"That's what I'm worried about," I said. "Jade alone with her thoughts." My chest started to knot up again. I probably should have told her I loved her before leaving her at the headquarters. I probably should have said sorry, too. I should have said a lot of things. But I didn't tell Dominic that. Instead, I said, "I probably should have brought her here. It would have kept her busy."

That drew Dominic's full attention, and he gave me a long, measured look. He jerked his chin up. "You screwed up again?"

I figured that was a fair statement. I'd pretty much screwed up everything when it came to Jade, but even so, I felt my jaw tick and clench. "She flipped out at her dad, and I might have thrown her over my shoulder and put her in the car to shut her up."

Dominic chuckled, his ice-blue eyes steady on mine, and he smirked. "Dude, really? Are you ever going to learn?"

I smirked back at him, watching his eyes dance with humor, as I folded my arms over my chest and shook my head. "She accused him of trying to protect his pack and then started shouting about how she'd be fighting alongside us when we attack them." My smile widened as I spoke, and I chuckled a little. Yeah, I would have preferred it if she hadn't freaked out, but I couldn't deny that I loved the passion I'd seen in her. Standing up for herself, for our pack. She'd been amazing.

"Oh," he said and blinked. "And I have no idea what to say about that." He stared at me as if he couldn't quite figure out how Jade could have done that, and then once he'd gotten over his shock, he frowned, looking disappointed, as if he were sad he'd missed it.

Dominic's eyes went back to Erika and held there for a second before coming back to me. "You need to pick a new head enforcer, and she needs a beta," he pointed out, not for the first time since I'd arrived. "And you need to figure out what you're going to do with the team."

I didn't particularly want to talk about the team, but I knew he was entirely right. I should have dealt with it before sending the guys out. Even if it was temporary, I should have appointed someone to lead them. But I hadn't. I'd followed my gut instead. Appointing someone would have taken time, discussion, and time wasn't something I'd wanted to waste.

As for the team themselves, I knew Jade would fight me on it if I even mentioned building a new one, and that was definitely not a fight I was looking forward to having with her.

I shook my head, frustrated, and rested my weight against the car. "Yeah, I know, Dom, but it really isn't my top priority right now."

The severe line of Dominic's mouth made it clear that he disagreed with me. "Well, it should be," he said, missing (or choosing) to ignore my frustration. "You can't send those guys out, leading the pack into this without a head. And you shouldn't have sent them anywhere today if you're not sure that you can trust them." He sighed, long and loud, rubbing a hand across his forehead. "You also need to stop worrying about Jade. She's going to be fine. She loves you. She's got your back in this. Trust me."

"You got someone in mind to head up the team?" I asked, ignoring his Jade advice and pasting on what was meant to be an open expression, encouraging him to go on.

He groaned, and damn, I almost laughed at the sound. Almost. Dominic's groans were a sure way to know what he was thinking, and this one was one that I got a lot. It was the *you're being a pain in the ass* groan, and he cut me a look that clearly said the same thing. Through his teeth, he said, "Tommy, if he'll stick around. The team could use someone experienced, and they seem to respect him."

"Tommy?" I asked blankly. I took in his expression. He was serious. Damn, he couldn't be serious. My phone rang, and I jammed my hand in my pocket, kind of glad for the interruption. I shook off the dread that had started to seep in at the thought of Tommy sticking around and said, "That's not his call, or mine," as I yanked my phone out. "My father would have to release him before I could even consider it."

Glancing down at my phone, I saw *Jade Shaw* flash across the screen and thumbed it quickly as I brought it to my ear. "Hi, sweetheart."

"Your girl's been sitting outside freezing her ass off since you left." The voice on the other end of the line was deep and rough and not Jade.

A hot rush of adrenaline hit me, and my hand flexed tight around the phone. "Who the hell is this?" I growled.

"Luken," the voice replied, rushed as if he were cluing into the fact that he probably should have led with that piece of information.

Cold swept through me, and more of that awful dread filled the pit of my stomach. Luken and Jade weren't close. They weren't even civil to each other. She wouldn't just give him her phone. I glanced at Dominic and mouthed *Luken.*His eyes darkened, and he jerked his chin toward the phone stuck to my ear, urging me to find out what was happening.

I pulled in a breath and asked as casually as I could, "Where's Jade?" Which, as it turned out, didn't come out casual at all.

"Just sent her inside," he blurted and then continued more slowly. "Her lips were turning blue. Also just had a little chat with her dad. Wants his daughter back home. Says he doesn't like the way you were treating her at his house, so he's willing to make a deal to get her back."

I laughed, a cold kind of laugh. Well, that hadn't taken long. "He can have her back when I'm in the ground."

"That might happen sooner than you think," Luken said coolly. "Once the team gets wind of you raising your hands to her, they'll come for you."

"You accusing me of something, Luken?" I asked, my voice, deathly calm.

"Did you hit her?" he fired at me, not missing a beat.

I ground my teeth. Furious didn't even come close to describing the heat that surged through me from his question. "Did it look like I hit her?"

"I figure you wouldn't drop her off here until she healed," he said. "And it would explain the thick fear in her scent and the nervous look she gave me when I told her I was going to give you a call."

"I didn't hurt her," I said through my teeth. "I wouldn't, and I'm pretty sure you already know that."

Luken hesitated for a second before continuing with what sounded like a whole lot of caution as if he weren't sure that he was free to speak his mind. "Then he's making a play. This could be our in. And by the way, your girl's having some issues when it comes to taking him out."

That was true. Jade was having some serious issues when it came to her father. But confirming that to a pack member that was not her number one fan most likely wouldn't go over well. So instead, I asked, "You know what the deal is?"

"Nope, he wants you to call him," he said. "All he said was that there's something big in play, something that you and Jade would want in on and that if you work with him, he won't tell anyone else about what he saw you do to her."

Okay, that was good. It was probably better that no one knew whatever it was that Jeff had to offer until I figured out what the hell he was up to. "Did Jade say anything?" I asked.

Luken didn't answer right away. He sighed, and let out a frustrated growl, then sighed again. When he spoke, his voice was strained. "She said a hell of a lot, but she doesn't know what he wants or what he's accusing you of. She didn't talk to him. I told her I'd run it by you and let you decide if she needed to know. She agreed to it, Aidan. Without hesitation. No argument. Nothing."

That wasn't so good. Jade being fully agreeable with Luken should have been good, but because it was Jade we talked about and he was, well, Luken, it really wasn't good. My jaw clenched, and through my teeth, I asked, "What's she doing now?"

"I sent her inside to see Marcy," he said with a huff. "She's freaked out, and she's pissed off. Not a good combination." He didn't quite manage to hide the bitterness from his tone.

Dominic's gaze was hard and unwavering, stuck on my face, and I inhaled slowly, attempting to work through the sudden irritation Luken's call had brought on and keep it out of my tone. The breath didn't help.

"Don't remember asking for your opinion," I bit out on a growl. I paused and took another breath. "Set up her phone to have her calls forwarded to me before you give it back to her." And with that, I dropped the call, not waiting for a confirmation.

"That was harsh," Dominic said evenly, and his lips twitched up at the corners.

I shoved my phone back in my pocket. "Your point?" I snapped, not seeing the humor in the situation. My eyes sparked. I felt the tingle, followed by a quick pulse of adrenaline.

"No point, just an observation," Dominic said in a low, calm voice, raising his hands. He waited for a beat, and when I didn't offer up anything, he asked, "You going to fill me in?"

I heaved a sigh, thought about telling him to screw off, but instead said, "Yeah." I pushed off the car, rolled my shoulders, and then quickly filled him in.

When I finished, Dominic didn't speak immediately. He was staring across the parking lot. I didn't need to wonder what he was thinking about. The torn, stricken expression gave him away. I was sure he was thinking the same things I was. How far would Jade go to end this? How much could we ask of her before she broke? And he was probably trying to decide if we should even tell her about the call.

He pulled in a shaky breath, blinked, and focused on me, his gaze resolved. "Call him. Set up a meeting."

"No," I said firmly. There was no way I would hand Jade back over to him. She was finally mine. All mine. There wasn't a chance in hell I'd give her up now, and honestly, we didn't need to. Jeff was scrambling. Trying to find some hold on us. I was sure of it.

He groaned long and loud, rubbing a hand roughly across his forehead. "Aidan, think about it. When the team hears about this, they'll freak."

I shook my head. "I'll handle the team," I said. "And I'm not negotiating with him. Not yet. We don't have any need to. We know where they are. My guess is he clued in that something was off when Jade lost it on him, and he's scrambling to get his foot back in with us."

"I don't think I agree with you," he said, but he was smiling. That smile faded as he said, "You going to tell her?"

"Yeah, I'll talk to her tonight." I dug my keys out of my pocket and rounded the car. I pulled the door open and paused. "Wrap things up here and meet me back at the headquarters. I want you and Mac to take her home. She needs some friend time."

"Will do," he said with a nod as I slid into the car. He watched me for a moment as I started it up, giving me a look that I didn't even try to understand, before dropping his gaze and stalking off toward Erika.

CHAPTER 5

JADE

The rain sounded more like hail beating against the window. The downpour had started about twenty minutes ago, and it didn't look like it would be letting up anytime soon. It was a soothing sound, so soothing it almost washed away all the nervous turmoil that was shifting through my belly. Almost.

I was sitting on the couch with a cozy light blue fleece tucked around me, wondering if the guys had made it back before the storm hit and waiting (a little impatiently) for Aidan to come home. It had been a couple of hours since he'd shown back up at the headquarters to find me passed out on the couch in his office. He'd woken me with a sweet press of his lips on my neck, which had led to an even sweeter press of his lips on mine, which then led to a kiss that was not sweet, but it was delicious.

Once he'd finished kissing me awake, he'd sent me home with Marcy and Dominic, claiming I needed some *friend time*. He didn't say a word about Luken's phone conversation with my father, and I hadn't asked. I also hadn't protested, not even a little, about needing *friend time*.

Now, though, I was kind of wishing I had.

"I'm telling you, you need to get a new beta," Dominic growled, not for the first time since we'd walk through the doors. He was getting annoyed at me, but then that wasn't really anything new. Dominic was usually annoyed at me for one thing or another.

I pulled in a deep breath through my nose and let it out slowly. "And I'm telling you I'm not ready to pick one." And it was true. I wasn't. It wasn't as if the first one I'd pick had turned out all that well, and with everything going on, well, I didn't think it was smart to rush into a decision like that.

Dominic groaned. It was his frustrated groan, short and abrupt, and he cut me a look that matched his groan. He was sitting in the big leather chair in the corner, knees spread and leaning forward, his elbows resting on his jean-clad thighs. His bleach-blond hair was, as always, spiked and gelled, and his blue eyes bore into me as he clenched and unclenched his jaw.

"Don't start with the groan fest, Dom," Marcy snapped. She was testy, too. She'd been testy since he'd picked us up at the headquarters and brought us back to Aidan's. "If she doesn't want a beta, then she doesn't have to pick one." She was curled up beside me, her feet pulled up underneath her, hugging her arms around her waist. Her hair was pulled back in a ponytail out of her face, and she had a soft gray fleece tucked around her.

"Stay out of this, Mac," Dominic growled and shot her a dirty look. "There's a lot at stake here."

"You think we don't know that?" she shrieked. She tossed her hands toward me in a dramatic gesture, and the fleece fell, pooling on her lap. "You think she doesn't get what's at stake?"

"I thought this was supposed to be *friend time*," I muttered, pulling my blanket up and tucking it under my chin. When Aidan had first suggested *friend time*, I'd pictured the three of us vegging out on the couch, watching a movie, eating junk food, and avoiding talking about anything that could lead to tears or arguments. What I did not picture was us fighting about whether or not I needed to pick a new beta.

Dominic looked at me, and whatever he saw made his eyes warm and soften, and when he spoke, his tone matched his eyes. "Honey, you've got to understand that when we move on them, everyone's going to be watching you. They can't be worried about having your back. They need to be focused. You having a beta will relieve some of that worry."

"Dom, please drop it," I said softly, dropping my burning eyes to my lap. "I know you're worried, and I'm sure you're right, but I just can't deal with this today." And I really couldn't. My brain, my body, every part of me was exhausted. "I'm not going to risk the pack, and I won't do anything to jeopardize my mate. I get what's at stake here probably better than anyone. My pack, my mate, my family. I'm going to lose something no matter what happens." I paused, swallowed down the burn that was creeping up my throat, and then huffed. "We can assign someone to stick close to me and let everyone know."

"Are you having second thoughts?" Marcy asked delicately, inching closer to me on the couch and pressing her shoulder to mine.

"No," I said with a certainty that I didn't even come close to feeling. "My father needs to be stopped. I'm just worried about Mom."

"The pack will look after her," Dominic said. "We'll take care of her."

I offered him a smile that really didn't feel anything like a smile. The burn in my throat started again, along with my eyes. I knew they would look after her. But knowing that didn't change anything. She would be devastated, and I found myself wondering if I should call her. I thought that if I were in her shoes, I'd want to know what was happening. I'd want some kind of warning. I'd want to know everything. If it were Aidan, I'd want to know that he was a monster.

Silence fell. It wasn't a comfortable silence, but I had to admit, it was a needed one. It was a breath of air, even if that air was thick and heavy and stale.

It was Marcy who broke it with a small laugh. She nudged my shoulder and asked, "You remember when we were eight, and your dad caught the three of us hiding in the crawlspace under your house?" She shook her head and smiled. "You swore you saw a cat crawl in there."

Dominic chuckled. "And I wanted to rescue it."

"You were going to grow up to be a superhero," I said, smiling a little. "God, your superhero phase lasted two years. You were trying to rescue everything, whether it needed rescuing or not."

Marcy giggled. "We used to stage trouble just so you could save us."

"I remember that day," Dominic said. He shook his head and grinned. "Your dad lost his mind when we crawled out with that damn skunk. I'll never forget the look on his face when it sprayed him." I laughed, and Dominic flashed me a big wide smile. "Still don't have a clue how we managed to pull it out without getting skunked ourselves."

AIDAN

Looking at them sitting on the couch in my office, I wondered how I never realized that the four of them were brothers. They might not look alike, but they had the same mannerisms. The way they sat, the way they held themselves, their facial expressions; it was all a lot of the same.

Tommy and Chris were propped against the wall by the door. They looked exhausted. Hell, we all were. It had been a long day, already closing in on 8:00.

After sending Jade home, my office had been a revolving door. I was pretty sure I'd had face time with every pack member, although after the fifth one had stormed in, everything had sort of blurred together. They'd all said something similar, confirming (heatedly) in one way or another that they were behind Jade and me, ready to fight for the pack and our territory.

I drummed my fingers on my desk, waiting for one of the guys to speak up, but they kept watching the door, waiting. Waiting for Jade to show up. The storm had blown in just before they got back, and the rain was coming down in sheets now. There was no way I was going to drag her out in it just to see the pain return to her eyes when she saw them again.

"She's at home with Mac and Dom," I muttered after another long beat of silence. "I'm not calling her to come in either. What did you guys find?"

Six sets of concerned eyes landed on me, all of them asking the same question, a question that I wasn't ready to hear the answer to. I rolled my hand impatiently, prompting them to start talking, and then resumed drumming my fingers. I was restless, so was my inner-wolf, and all I could think about was going home. I needed — we all needed — this day to end.

"I counted twenty," Beck spoke up. For a split second, he looked disgusted before his face hardened. "Plus three kids. One girl, two boys. But we couldn't get close enough. There could be more."

Shit. I stilled my fidgety hand, only to drag it across

my face and through my hair. Kids. *Shit!* Of course, there'd be kids. The women were there to be used, to breed males for them.

"The girl ..." I started and then paused, swallowing down a rush of bile that gathered in my throat. My inner-wolf pressed against my chest, and I bit the inside of my lip, tamping down the urge to let him out. "Was she ...?"

"She looked young," Mark said, but he didn't sound sure. "Too young. Maybe fourteen."

"They were smiling and laughing with her," Landon added. He sounded stunned as if he weren't sure he could believe what he'd seen. "They were playing with her. I don't think ..." He shook his head, letting his words fall short, and his frown deepened.

"Good." I nodded, although it sure as hell didn't sound good, but I found myself repeating, "Good. What about the boys? Any idea on their ages?"

"Toddlers," Tommy said. "Still in diapers."

I nodded. "Okay," I said and swallowed hard. "Anything else? Security? Lookouts?"

"There was no security, at least none that I could see," Craig said. "They seemed pretty relaxed, barbequing, drinking. I'm going to guess that Jeff isn't on to us. I figure they'd be on alert if he was."

"Or he is on to us and doesn't want us to know," I said, meeting each one of them in the eyes, searching for anything that showed they were holding something back — something that Tommy or Chris might not have noticed — but I didn't see or scent anything off. "He called after we dropped off the body. He wants Jade to move back home."

"Good for him. She won't be doing it," Beck bit out. His gaze darkened with anger. "What did she have to say about it?"

I sighed and raked a hand through my hair. "She

doesn't know yet. Luken took the call, and I guess she was pretty upset, so he told her he'd talk to me, let me decide if she needed to know or not." Beck let out a laugh, and I held up my hand to keep him from saying what we were all thinking. "She agreed with him, guys. She didn't fight it. No argument. She even walked away so he could call me."

I quickly filled them in on the conversation, telling them about Luken's accusations and about Jeff's admittance that there was more going on than we thought. The entire time I spoke, I waited for one of them to snap because Luken was right. I was sure that if one of them thought that I'd actually hit her, they'd be all over me for it. Jade was, after all, one of theirs. She wasn't just their alpha female. As far as they were concerned, she was part of their team, and they loved her like a little sister.

But they didn't snap. Actually, I thought they even looked a little sorry for me, which was kind of weird.

"She okay?" Landon asked, concerned when I finished.

"Honestly," I said, shaking my head. "I don't know." I pushed my chair back, standing up. "Go home, guys. Get some sleep. I've got to go fill her in." I stepped around my desk and headed for the door. "Let's meet for breakfast tomorrow, all of you. Be at the diner for eight."

CHAPTER 6

JADE

My belly hurt, and I felt like I was about to pee myself, but I couldn't stop laughing. Each time I thought I was almost done, and I tried to catch my breath, Dominic or Marcy would start, and their laughter would set me off again. It was like a chain reaction; one of us started, and it caught on to all of us.

I wrapped my arms around my stomach, trying to hold myself together as my body shuddered through the side-splitting laughter. It hurt so much, but I had to admit, it also felt really darn good.

The skunk had definitely been the highlight of our summer that year.

Aidan crashed through the front door, which flung back and hit the wall with a startling boom, and then he slammed it shut. I jumped — literally jumped — flying off the couch, my heart in my throat.

"I hate rain," he muttered, wiping his face on his soaking wet sleeve. He was soaked through, his hair plastered to his head, and water running down his face and neck. He pulled off his jacket, and it fell to the floor with a watery smack.

"You scared the crap out of me," I muttered. He

looked a little pissed off and really tired, and he continued to curse the storm under his breath, not even looking up at us.

My lips started to twitch as I watched him shuck off his water-filled sweater, and I swear I tried seriously hard to hold it back, but then he mumbled something that sounded like, *Stupid damn rain* and a burst of laughter tumbled out of me. And with that, Marcy and Dominic started howling right along with me.

Aidan snapped his gaze up, focused on mine. He looked a little shocked to see us all watching him, but the shock didn't last. He lifted a brow. "Something funny?" His voice was growled, but his lips were curving up at the corners.

I tried really hard to straighten my face and gave him my best serious look, which probably wasn't all that serious since I was still giggling. I shook my head. "Nope. Nothing funny." I darted over to him, went up on my toes, and planted a sloppy wet kiss on his cheek. He chuckled, and I swore he looked relieved. He reached out for me, and I managed to duck away before he could pull me into a soggy hug and called, "I'll grab you a towel," as I shot for the stairs.

By the time I got back downstairs with a towel, Aidan was down to his boxers, which only looked a little damp, leaning against the wall in the entryway. Dominic and Marcy were at the door, pulling on their jackets.

"You guys don't have to go yet," I said. "You can wait out the rain if you want or crash here." I padded across the room, and the minute I reached Aidan, his hand came out, wrapping around my wrist and pulling me in tight to his side. He plucked the towel out of my hand and rubbed it along his hair without letting me go.

Marcy smiled. "I promised Trevor I'd be home," she said and giggled. "And I think your man wants some attention." She pulled open the door, and she visibly shuddered as she looked out at the rain. "Is it unlocked?" she asked, looking back at Dominic. He nodded, and she said, "See you tomorrow, guys," and with a little wave, she ran out to the car.

Dominic held back for a moment, giving Aidan one of those expectant *start talking* kind of looks. I glanced up at Aidan, saw his frown and the slight shake of his head, and he said, "Give Tommy a call and get him to fill you in."

Dominic frowned. He held Aidan's gaze for a minute and then nodded. "Sure," he said, but he didn't sound happy about it. "See you guys tomorrow." And then he stepped outside, shut the door, and it was just Aidan and me.

Aidan was quiet, stroking a hand absently up and down my back, seemingly content to stand in the entryway holding me. His gaze was on the door, but I didn't really think he was seeing anything. He looked lost, buried under the weight of his thoughts.

"Everything okay?" I asked, shifting in his arms and eyeing him carefully, the same way he watched me.

Aidan smiled a little and caressed my cheek. "Not sure how to answer that, sweetheart. A lot of shit happened today." He leaned into me, pressing a soft kiss on my lips, and said, "I need a shower. Why don't you go get ready for bed? We'll talk when I'm done, okay?"

"Yeah, sure," I said, but I wrapped my arms around his waist, holding him to me, and inhaled a deep lungful of his scent.

He chuckled. "I won't be long. Promise." He gave me another quick kiss, a tight squeeze, and reluctantly, I let him go.

I stood there for a long moment after he vanished upstairs, just listening to the rain pelt against the window. I don't know how long I stood there waiting to feel the nerves that I was sure had to be just itching to fill my belly. I thought I should probably be nervous. Aidan was most likely going to tell me what my dad wanted and what the guys found out. But oddly enough, I wasn't. Maybe it was the *friend time,* maybe it relaxed me, or maybe I was just exhausted, but I felt stable for the first time today. Solid.

I made my way upstairs and paused, hovering outside the bathroom for a second, thinking again that at any moment, I would feel the nerves, but again, nothing. So I moved on and did what Aidan asked. I got ready for bed.

After changing into a tank top and pajama shorts, I curled up in bed. I must have dozed off because the next thing I knew, I was jumping at the creak of the door hinges.

Aidan chuckled softly. "Tired?" he asked as he walked over to the dresser. He rummaged around in the top drawer and pulled out a pair of plaid pajama pants.

"Yeah, I guess I am," I said. His back was to me, and I thought I should probably look away as he dropped his towel, but um … well, I didn't. Instead, my gaze wandered along the muscular plains of his back, watching them ripple as he stepped into the pants and tugged them on.

He turned, catching me watching him, and smirked that sexy half-smirk. I wasn't really sure how I managed it, but I rolled my eyes at him, and somehow I didn't blush, not even a little at being caught.

Aidan's eyes never swayed from mine as he crossed over to the bed. He climbed in beside me, his arm went around my waist, pulling my front snug against his side, and I rested my cheek on his chest.

Once he had me situated where he wanted me, he let

out a slow breath and said, "Your dad's making a play. That call Luken took, well, he wants you to move back home. He even went as far as saying that I hit you."

"Okay," I said, not sure what else to say. There was nothing, absolutely nothing that he could do to make me move back there, and his accusation was a joke. Aidan wouldn't hit me. He just wouldn't. "Um ... did you talk to him?"

"No. I'm not negotiating with him." Aidan's muscles were tense, jumping and twitching, and I rubbed my cheek against his chest, waiting for him to say more. His response made no sense to me. I wasn't arguing with him. I wasn't even acknowledging Dad's ludicrous accusation, yet, he was tense. Stressed. Wound up tight.

He made a noise from the back of his throat that sounded like a mix between a growl and a sigh. "The guys reported in, too." He paused, stiffened further, and then sighed, relaxing a little. "Your dad's pack has kids with them. A girl and two boys."

"What?" I went to sit up, but his arm tightened around me, holding me against his chest, not loosening until I stopped moving.

I held still, waiting for him to elaborate, but he didn't. He ran a hand through my hair and said, "We're meeting the guys for breakfast tomorrow, and if it goes well, we'll be going in for those kids immediately."

I blinked and tried to sit up again, but it was a useless effort. He held me tight against him. His breathing was strained, his heart thumping quickly against my cheek. It was then that I clued into what this was. He was reporting to me. He didn't want to talk it all out right then. He didn't want me to get upset. He was probably still worried I couldn't take anymore today, but he knew he had to keep me looped in.

So instead of telling him exactly what I thought

about the little breakfast meeting tomorrow and demanding answers, I asked, "And if it doesn't go well?" My tone, unfortunately, came out sharper than I would have liked.

He noticed it, and his arms tightened again. Taking a deep breath and slowly letting it out, he loosened his hold but didn't let go. His fingers continued to shift through my hair, and when he spoke, his voice was firm. "I'll be picking a new team and then going in for the kids."

I listened to his words, heard his tone, and realized that I was completely wrong. It wasn't that he didn't want to talk it out. He'd already made his decisions, and he was simply telling me what the plan was. I pressed my face harder against his chest, trying to get closer, show him that I wasn't going to pull away, no matter what, and said, "Aidan, you can't ..."

"Jade, sweetheart, they betrayed me," he said, cutting me short. "They betrayed you. I can't risk that happening again. Not with this."

I opened my mouth and then snapped it shut because I couldn't exactly argue with that. He was right. No matter how much I didn't want it to be true, the team had betrayed us. "I'm with you, Aidan, and I swear I'm not as breakable as you think."

He leaned forward, pressing his lips to my hair. "I know, sweetheart."

I lay there, my cheek pressed against his chest, running a lazy trail with my fingertips along the ridges of his abs as I tried to process everything, which really wasn't working out too well. My brain was fried. I was exhausted. Processing tonight wasn't looking like a viable option.

Aidan shifted beside me, placing his hands on my hips, and pulled me up onto his body. His lips moved from my hair to my cheek, down my face, along my jaw, and settled at my neck. His tongue flicked out, teasing the sensitive skin below my ear.

Heat rushed over my skin and pooled in my belly as a whisper-soft moan pushed past my lips.

He rolled, trapping me beneath his hard body, staring straight into my eyes. "I forgot to tell you something earlier," he murmured. He planted his forearms on the bed, holding most of his weight off of me, and his hands came up, framing my face.

"What's that?" I asked and squirmed against his chest, my heart plummeting. I didn't think I wanted to hear anymore, at least not tonight. What I wanted was more of his kisses. More of the heat, the contact. Something good to cover up the bad.

He caressed my cheek with his thumb and lowered his head, pressing his lips to mine. "I love you, Jade."

My heart danced in my chest. I opened my mouth to tell him the same but didn't get the chance. His lips pressed down on mine, and his tongue was inside my mouth, tasting, exploring. His hand slipped into my hair, wrapping it around his fist, and he pulled me closer, still.

I locked my arms around him, holding him close. The feeling of his skin against mine was perfect, and my body began to pulse with heat. I exhaled when his lips left mine and fluttered down my neck, below my ear, and dipped down to flutter across my shoulder, feeling some of the day's tension and stress fall from me, only to be replaced with a whole new wonderful kind of tension.

Aidan gave me the heat and the contact that I'd wanted, and I had to say, it was way better than *something good*. And it was exactly what I needed.

CHAPTER 7

AIDAN

My inner-wolf stirred within my chest, and I woke up slowly, chasing a dream that I couldn't quite grasp onto. The fading sounds of wolves howling in the night drifted in and out as the dream dissolved into a groggy, disjointed memory.

I blinked, clearing the sleepy film that layered my eyes. The storm was still going strong, crashing against the house. Rain beat against the windows; thunder rumbled throughout the sky. A flash of lightning lit up my bedroom and then faded, shrouding me once again in darkness. The only light left was coming from the red glow of the digital alarm clock that sat on the nightstand beside me, telling me it was 1:03 in the morning.

Uneasiness unfurled in my gut, and I scrubbed at my face. That dream. The sound of my pack, baying and chasing and tearing into flesh, shifted throughout my conscious mind as if it had been real. It felt real. Sounded real.

Jade was curled up beside me, and as always, she had me right at the edge of the mattress. Her forehead was pressed into my shoulder, and she had an arm thrown over my belly. Her eyes were closed, and her breathing was steady. She was smiling, just a little upward tilt at the corners of her mouth. Peaceful. Content.

A clap of thunder rattled the windows, and I sighed as I listened to it rumble through the sky and fade into the distance. I rubbed at my face again. It was nothing. Just a dream. Probably my subconscious preparing for the inevitable fight my pack was about to embark on. And with that thought, I closed my eyes and drifted back to sleep.

A chorus of howls broke through my sleepy brain, and my eyes snapped open again. That wasn't a dream. I was sure of it. My inner-wolf shifted and stirred again within my chest. He was agitated, urging me up, begging me to move and see what was happening.

I lay still, straining my hearing, waiting, listening ... The wolves' howls sounded again, and I quickly lifted Jade's arm from my stomach and slipped out of bed, careful not to wake her. The muscles in the side of her cheek flexed, and she rolled, flopping onto her back and throwing her arms out wide, before settling back into steady, even breathing.

I felt around the floor, searching for the pajama pants I'd tossed earlier that night. After a moment of searching, I found them at the foot of the bed, tangled with the sheets, and tugged them on before easing out of the room.

My wolves were close. As I crept down the staircase, avoiding the creaking third step from the top, I could smell traces of them. With the rain pounding relentlessly, they had to be within feet of the house for me to pick up their scent. It was watery, weak, and diluted, but it was there. Their baying grew louder. It was excited and frenzied and close. Too close.

In a heartbeat, I leaped down the remaining steps and hurried to the door. Through the small window,

I saw a flash of white. The howling stopped abruptly only to be replaced by a low, menacing growl.

I yanked the door open, bolting out into the pouring rain. Air pounded in and out of my lungs in harsh pants. My heart ratcheted up, tripling in beats as I inhaled sharply. Rain. Dead leaves. Blood. Wolves. Green. Bitter. Birchbark. Cougar. The scents assaulted me, and I started to breathe faster and faster as I searched the front yard for any sign of the sources.

The howling started again, coming from the side of the house, getting closer and closer. Paws smacked against the wet ground, the sound almost inaudible over the rain, and suddenly, a mess of beasts, wolves, and cougars, shot past my front deck. My gaze zeroed in on a white wolf — Luken — as he took a leap, tackling one of the cougars. They rolled through the sodden grass, flipping over a few times before springing free from each other again.

Shit! I glanced back at the house as a wave of heat pulsed from within me. All my thoughts centered on Jade. I had to keep her safe. I had to keep them away from her while she slept.

I reached out and pulled the door closed. My skin shuddered, and I started to feel a little shaky from all the adrenaline that pumped through my veins. The shift was coming quickly — quicker than normal — my inner-wolf was jerking against my skin. He wanted out. He needed to protect our mate.

I kicked off my pants. Coarse hair layered my skin. My bones snapped, cracked, lengthened, twisted. I snarled, and my inner-wolf sprang free.

The rain was freezing against my fur-coated skin, soaking me through. I moved to the edge of the deck, tracking the movements of my pack as they tangled with the feline beasts. With a quick scan through the downpour, I counted fifteen wolves and seven ... no ... six cougars.

My wolves were all over the place. There was no center, no organization. They looked as if they were simply reacting to each attack. I didn't understand it. They were struggling, not seeming to gain any ground even with the greater numbers. The cougars were darting around them, quick and efficient, almost as if they were taunting them.

I barked and let my scent thicken in the air, hoping to draw their focus, and I instantly noticed the change in my wolves. Their movements went from sloppy and erratic to alert, and they began to fall into groups, protecting each other's backs and pushing the cougars toward the tree line.

One of the cougars broke off, stalking in my direction. My hackles rose, and the hair along my spine stood on end. The solid, beige-colored cat was large, coming close to my height in wolf form. He was built with sleek muscles, his shoulders packed and powerful. His eyes, a bright green, rimmed with black, were fixed on me.

He stopped a few feet from the deck and hissed. A flash of lightning struck through the black sky, and I caught sight of his long, razor-sharp fangs. He pawed at the muddy ground, growling, and hissing.

My lips curled, and I snarled. I wanted to jump down and tear into the monster, but I couldn't bring myself to move, even for a second, and leave Jade unprotected and sleeping in the house. How did they get this far into town? We'd known that they were coming closer, circling houses on the outskirts, but not this far in. Not with us constantly watching.

Suddenly he leaped at me, a powerful thrust from his hind legs propelling him forward, and before I could move, his fangs struck, burying into my shoulder. I pivoted, tossing him off balance, and just as quickly as he was on me, the cougar was back on the ground a few feet from the deck, hissing again.

My snarl was drowned out by a clap of thunder. My shoulder felt as if it were on fire. A streak of lightning chased through the night, and I saw the big cat push off again, launching toward me.

I shimmied back a couple steps, and as he hit the wooden planks of the deck, I leaped on him. The animal's knees buckled, and he fell to his belly. My heart was pounding in my ears, drowning out the sounds of the fights breaking out around me as I stared down at the cat below me. I bared my teeth, and went to bury them in his neck when I realized that he wasn't fighting, wasn't trying to push me off.

Shit! He was submitting. The beast within me wanted him to struggle, to give me a reason to end his sad little life, but he stayed still. He made a sound that sounded a hell of a lot like a laugh, and he started to shift.

I backed up off him, and he rolled up to his knees. He was older. Probably mid-forties, with a pot-belly and beady black eyes. He had a full head of black hair and a thick salt and pepper beard. He held out his hands, showing surrender, but he never once lowered his eyes from mine.

I noticed my pack was closing in around us from the corner of my eye. With a quick glimpse up, I saw a lump of beige fur about ten feet away lying motionless, and the rest of the cougars were gone.

Disgust rose up around me as I turned my focus back to the man in front of me. His pack abandoned him without even a thought, leaving him at our mercy.

I shifted and rose up to my feet, towering over him. He looked up, a cruel smile on his face, and he laughed.

"You should have killed me," the man said, his voice higher than I expected.

Probably, I thought. He deserved death, even if it was only because he came into my territory and attacked me. My aching, bloody shoulder was proof of that. It was enough to end his life, whether he showed signs of submission or not. And if he hadn't shifted, I would have ended him, but it felt sickeningly wrong to do it while he was human. While he had no chance of defending himself.

I gritted my teeth, glowering down at him. "Not sure how you do this in your pack, but here, once someone submits and shifts, we don't kill."

"Pathetic." The man laughed. "Just for the record, I would have killed you." He laughed again, muttering something about me being weak, and then said, "I shifted to give you a message. The girl needs to be with her family, and we will take her back."

Growls erupted, and my wolves stalked closer. Clearly, the bastard had no sense of self-preservation because he started to shift, his face reshaping into that of a large cat. Long fangs descended first, slowly, as if he were taunting me, and then his bones began to break.

Luken was on him as his shift finished, not giving him a chance to run. The others were snarling and snapping around us, ready to take him down. But they didn't need to be. The meaty sound of flesh tearing, ripping, pulling, filled my ears as I watched Luken's white coat stain crimson. The cougar screamed a high-pitched sound that ripped through the air, and then his body went limp.

Jeff sent his cougars in the middle of the night to collect Jade. At that moment, that was the only thought I had. The girl the cougar had been talking about was Jade.

I had no doubt about that, and the knowledge rattled me to my core.

I closed my eyes, sucking in breath after breath. The rain felt like pebbles smacking against my bare flesh, stinging my skin. My wolves had quieted, now that the threat was gone, but I could feel them watching me, waiting.

"Aidan, what's going on?" Jade's voice came from behind me, and I spun around. "I heard howling and a scream." She was standing in the doorway wearing only one of my hoodies that hung mid-thigh on her, rubbing sleep from her eyes. Her hands dropped. She paled as she looked past me, most likely at the wolves who were still growling. She turned a little gray as she looked down, spotting the dead cougar on our deck, and then her eyes came up and landed on my shoulder, and her expression changed from sick to concern. "Jesus, what happened?"

"I'm fine," I said, my voice sounding rough and growled. "Just a small flesh wound." I shook my head and stepped toward her. Rainwater dripped from my arms as I lifted a hand to her cheek. The thought of telling her to go inside crossed my mind. She'd been through hell today, and she didn't need anymore, but I couldn't do it. She needed to know, and there was no way I would start hiding things from her again. "It looks like your dad was serious about wanting you home. And I'm thinking he's done with pretending to have an alliance with us."

The sound of bones snapping and reshaping drew Jade's attention from me. I dropped my hand from her face and turned to find Luken, blood caked around his mouth and on his chest, rising to his feet.

He opened his mouth, but I lifted a hand to silence him. "How the hell did they get this close?" I demanded. "And where is the team?"

"Aidan," Jade said softly, her tone, her scent, both urged me to calm down, and I took a deep breath, holding my fury at bay. The other wolves backed up a few steps, dropping their muzzles to the ground. Not one of them shifted, most likely so they wouldn't have to answer me.

Luken cleared his throat, and he looked as if he were regretting not staying in wolf form. "The team ..." he looked down to his toes, let out a breath, and whispered, "We tried to call them when we first spotted the cougars, but we couldn't reach them. The cougars came straight here, Aidan. They knew where they were going."

"I'll call Beck," Jade offered, and she started to shuffle back into the house.

"No," I barked way too harshly, and I instantly felt sick. I turned to her. Her eyes were wide with surprise. "Sorry, sweetheart," I muttered. "Leave them for tonight. We'll talk to them in the morning about it."

Her face fell. She knew exactly what that meant. That I hadn't changed my mind about chatting with them. And I thought she got that not answering a call during an attack seriously didn't help their case. She must have thought it, too, because she didn't argue and nodded in agreement, looking grim but resolved.

She looked back to Luken. "Did anyone else get hurt?" she asked. She was making a conscious effort to keep her eyes on our faces. I could see it in the stiffness of her neck and the stillness of her eyes. There was a slight blush coloring her cheeks, and I thought that it was kind of cute. Even with an animal dead on our deck, she was still acutely aware that she was standing in front of two naked men.

Luken's nostrils flared, and I was sure he was picking up the scent of Jade's unease. It was a tangy smell and hung thick in the air. He shifted from foot to foot, nervously, and looked back at the wolves, gathered around us. "A few scratches," he said after a moment. "Nothing that won't heal. There's another dead cougar on the lawn."

"Can you and the others deal with this?" she asked, waving a hand toward the dead cougar. "And the other one? I want to look at his shoulder."

"Yeah, sure," he said, and he looked at me as if he wanted me to confirm his order.

"Thought we were past this, Luken," I said, my gaze hard and cold, so was my tone. "She gave you an order."

Luken threw up his hands and backed up a step. "I didn't mean any offense. It's just her scent," he said. "It's uncertain. Uneasy."

I chuckled, my anger dissolving. "It's because we're naked," I said and smirked back at Jade. "You really have to get over that, sweetheart."

Jade gave me an adorable dirty look before forcing a smile on Luken. "Sorry, still not used to all of this." She sighed and hugged her arms around her waist, shifting her weight to her right foot. "Bring the dead back to the headquarters." She moved her gaze to my face and blushed a little more. "I want to give them back to my dad, but I don't want my mom there when we do it."

I gave her a little smile. "Sounds like a plan, sweetheart."

CHAPTER 8

JADE

"This is a waste of time, Aidan," I said and swallowed down the rusty taste of guilt that gathered in my mouth. I pulled in a deep breath and shut my eyes for a second. That shivery, breakable feeling filled my chest again. I wasn't one-hundred percent sure exactly where the horrid feeling was stemming from because, well, Aidan wasn't entirely wrong, but I felt it nonetheless.

The feeling first crept in last night, or I guess technically it was this morning, right after we'd left the pack to deal with the dead cougars. While I'd cleaned out the deep gouges that the cougar had left in his shoulder and watched as it healed, Aidan explained why he didn't want me to call Beck, which basically that they should have been there to start with. He then told me he was exhausted, walked me to bed, pulled me into his arms, and returned to sleep promptly. Surprisingly enough, I fell asleep with him. I didn't know what to make of that, but I thought that it probably had something to do with the fact that I was emotionally tapped out and couldn't bring myself to feel anything about the attack one way or another.

When he woke me up for the second time this morning, he'd been all business, laying out exactly how he felt about the team. He'd explained again why we hadn't called them about the little cougar hiccup that had happened on our front deck last night. I tried to reason with him, telling him that the guys were probably sleeping when Luken had tried them the first time, but Aidan had managed to poke holes in that logic. They were werewolves. They had awesome hearing. The phone ringing would have woken them up. When I tried to say that maybe they'd turned off their phones or at least turned off the ringers, I only managed to make matters worse for the guys. The enforcers always needed to be reachable, so turning off their phones was just as bad as not answering the call.

And not answering the call last night had made Aidan's doubt grow. He needed to be sure about them. Sure that they were loyal. So I'd listened to him and argued my points, but in the end, he stood firm, and I'd relented, agreeing that the meeting was probably a good idea.

Aidan took my hand in his and threaded our fingers together. "We've been over this, Jade," he said, sounding more than a little exasperated. "We're just going to talk to them." He tugged on my hand, pulling me with him as he started across the parking lot.

Dragging my heels, I followed, dreading every single step we took closer to the doors. *Talk to them* was code for deciding whether or not the team still had a future within the pack. Okay, maybe that wasn't entirely right. They would always have a place in Dog Mountain with the pack, just maybe not as enforcers.

I hadn't told Aidan outright, but there was a chance (a teeny, tiny chance) that his concerns were valid. Even though, in the end, the guys had stepped up and done the right thing, they'd also played us. They'd helped Jared. They'd wanted revenge. And if it weren't for the fact that they'd found out that Jared had known where the cougars were, I was pretty sure they would have helped him further or at least continued to turn a blind eye to what he'd been doing. And yeah, it really didn't look good that they'd been called last night and had been unreachable. So I completely got where Aidan was coming from on this issue.

But still, they'd turned over their brother. Their flesh and blood. Even though they knew that he would die for his crimes against the pack.

This morning, the sun was bright, almost too bright, after yesterday's dreary day. The parking lot shimmered, still wet from the storm. In some places, the rain had frozen, leaving a slippery ultra-thin layer of ice on the concrete.

I glanced up at him, squinting against the glare. "Aidan," I said and paused, waiting for a beat, before asking, "Why are you pushing this? They've proven their loyalty to you — to us. What's talking to them going to change?"

Aidan gave me a long, serious look. "I need to be sure. There's too much at stake here. We can't move on your dad without knowing if they'll turn on us again." He paused and let out a slow breath. "I can't trust your judgment when it comes to them, Jade. You care about them too much, and you've been wrong about them before."

His comment stung for a moment. Neither of us would say it out loud, but the whole trust thing was still a raw issue between us. He must have noticed my small wince because right then, I caught a sliver of regret that seeped into his expression. The sliver grew, quickly turning into deep, pained lines that spread like vines from the corners of his eyes, and I knew, just knew that he wasn't trying to hurt me with his words.

Those lines were getting deeper each time they appeared, and seeing them hurt my heart. I knew he was blaming himself for not noticing what Jared had been up to, for not stopping it before it ended in death. He hated himself for taking someone else from the guys, and he figured that if he hated himself, then they must hate him, too. He told me as much in the shower this morning, just before shutting the topic down and refusing to talk about it.

"They don't blame you," I murmured and pulled him to a stop just outside the door of the diner. I stepped in front of him, searching his eyes, but they gave nothing away other than regret.

Aidan watched me with an intense focus. He'd opted for jeans and a blue and gray striped button-down shirt that he'd left un-tucked. His hair was in its usually carefree mess, and he'd left a day's growth of stubble shadowing his jawline.

"Maybe not," he said with a calm remoteness. "But they hid their blame once, and I'm not going to risk it again."

I nodded, a few fast bobs of my head, not trusting my voice. His detachment, the way he closed me off, hiding everything behind that calm mask, felt like a physical slap, and the intensity of his stare made me wonder if it wasn't just the guys he was worrying about. "I don't ..." I started and then stopped, clearing the prickly lump from my throat. "I don't blame you either." It came out hoarse and whisper-quiet. God, my emotions were going haywire. They had been all over the place since I woke up, and it was driving me batty. His coolness wasn't a personal attack. Logically, I knew that. He was dealing with his demons, but no matter how much my head knew that, my heart didn't want to believe it.

A sad smile played at the corners of his mouth.

There was something else in his gaze that I couldn't even begin to understand as he tugged on my hand, pulling me against him. He coiled his arms around me, and I tucked my head in the crook of his neck, breathing in the clean scent of soap and his crisp, sweet aroma of greens, as he pressed a kiss on the top of my head. "I love you, Jade."

"I love you, too," I said. I lifted my head and placed a light kiss on his neck, swallowing down the breakable feeling that was gathering again. His skin felt like velvet against my lips, and although I wanted to stay put, I forced myself out of his arms. If he needed to be sure that the guys were behind him, then I'd give him that. I had to give him that even if it was tearing me up to do it. I leaned in and pecked him lightly on the cheek, avoiding his arms as he tried to capture me again, and pushed the door open with confidence that I really didn't feel.

Inside, the diner was busy, just as I'd hoped. I'd figured the public place would help keep everyone's tempers in check. The place looked warm and inviting with large leather-covered booths and bright lights. The waitress hustled about, and the room was alive with the early breakfast rush chatter.

The waitress greeted us with a bright smile as she rushed forward. She ushered us to a secluded booth in the back corner, chattering away about the day's specials. She was a couple of years older than me, and for the life of me, I couldn't remember her name. Connie ... Corinne ... something like that. She blushed a lot as she spoke and brushed up against Aidan even more as we made our way through the restaurant.

When we reached our table, the team was already there, looking deadly and gorgeous. But despite them looking amazing, there was something dark and lethal in their eyes. I saw it the moment Aidan sat down, and it made my stomach sink a little.

As soon as we were seated, the waitress filled up our water glasses and took our drink orders, oblivious to the silent tension shifting around our table. She smiled, a cheery and more than a little excited smile, and then she rushed off to fill our orders.

"Where's Tommy and Chris?" Aidan asked. His tone was cool, so was his body language, and I nudged him in the ribs, hoping he'd chill out.

"Don't know," Craig said. He smiled a forced smile. He was breathing hard, his nostrils flaring. I thought he was probably trying to pick up the scent of our emotions, and when his eyes fell on me, they frosted over, and his jaw clenched tight.

And it hurt. The team, not a single one of them, looked at me like that. It was as if Craig knew I was about to betray them. I was pretty sure that they all knew. I snagged up a menu, seriously not liking his scrutiny.

Aidan didn't comment on the *don't know* answer, but I felt him stiffen beside me. He dug out his phone and fired off a quick text before placing it on the table.

I kept quiet for a moment, waiting for someone to speak up, but no one did. The tension at our table was building so high that I could barely concentrate on the menu in front of me.

"I'm starving." My voice was overly bright and cheery, and I cringed on the inside hearing it. If my cluttered scent hadn't given away my guilt, I was certain that my voice had. "I think I'm going to get ..."

Landon reached across the table, pushing the menu I was hiding behind down. "You talk to your dad yet?" he asked, eyeing me curiously. His lips curved in a weary smile as he glanced at Aidan and took in my mate's stressed-out vibes.

I shook my head, trying to bring his attention back to me. "No, not yet. We thought ..."

"Jade," Aidan said in warning, stopping me short. His hand went to my thigh, squeezing a little, and I bit my tongue.

The guys sat up a bit straighter, watching us. There was a bit of confusion in their gazes as if they weren't entirely sure why Aidan was cutting me off, but I could also see that they weren't entirely surprised by it either.

"We're not here to discuss how to get those kids out, are we?" Beck asked through his teeth. "What's this about?" His blue eyes clouded with a layer of palpable pain, and his lips were tight as he spoke.

Aidan leaned back in the booth and stretched his arm behind me along the top, letting his hand hang down to graze against my shoulder. His fingertips traced lazy lines, back and forth along the side of my neck as he said, "Nope. I'm giving you a chance to convince me that she's right about you guys."

"Aidan," I hissed, elbowing him again. That was definitely harsher than necessary. That shivery guilt made another appearance, and I pulled in a deep breath, trying to tamp it down.

"Jade, don't," Aidan said softly before I could say anything else. "It's better this way. Blunt and open. We all need to be on the same page here if this is going to work."

There was a breath of silence, and I found myself under the scrutiny of four sets of eyes, and then, after a crazy long minute, Landon finally chuckled. "Haven't you learned anything in the last few days?" he asked with a wide, carefree kind of grin aimed at Aidan. "Jade's always right, even when she's wrong."

I rolled my eyes at him and snorted out a strained laugh. "I'm never wrong."

That earned me a round of chuckles, and I pursed

my lips, waiting for their laughter to stop. When it did, I opened my mouth and closed it without saying anything because the waitress scurried over with a tray full of orange juice and coffee. She took her sweet time placing the drinks on the table, casting flirty, mega-watt smiles as she did it. She took our food orders just as slowly, and then, with another round of bright smiles, she finally left.

I poured three big spoons full of sugar into my coffee and stirred, letting my spoon clink against the mug. "Guys, what Aidan was trying to say is that we thought maybe we should disband the team and build a new one. One that doesn't have blood ties to each other or the last alpha."

"Some of us might have wanted to see you crash and burn," Beck said to Aidan as if he were the one who had spoken. He reached for a creamer, opened it, and dumped it into his coffee. "But we're loyal to the pack. You know that. We've proven that to you."

Aidan nodded. "Yeah, you have. But you've also proven that you can be swayed, and I can't risk that happening again."

Landon lifted his shoulders in a lazy shrug. "Do what you need to do, man," he said. "We won't fight it."

"That's it?" Aidan asked. He sounded surprised, and honestly, I didn't know why. They weren't the *talk about your feelings* type. Honestly, I was just happy it was going better than I thought it would. No one was yelling or growling. Eyes weren't flaring, and I didn't see any skin shudders. They might have looked pissed off, but at least they were keeping their inner-wolves in check.

Craig slammed his coffee cup down, the contents sloshing up over the side. "Did you expect us to beg?"

There goes staying calm, I thought more than a little

bitterly. I glanced around quickly, hoping no one noticed the rise in Craig's voice and was glad to find no eyes staring in our direction.

Mark swore softly and cut his brother a look that clearly said, *shut up.* Craig saw it. He merely lifted his shoulders in a shrug and gulped water.

"No, I didn't." Aidan sighed. "She sees something good in you guys. I'm just trying to see it, too."

"Aidan," I snapped, and I cut him a dirty look. "You're not making this easy."

"Don't think there's a way to make this easy," said Mark. He reached across the table, took my hand, and gave it a little squeeze. He held his gaze steady on mine. "What do you think about all this?"

That was a good question, and I didn't answer right away, taking a minute to gather my thoughts. When I spoke, I kept my voice at a whisper, making sure no one would overhear. "I think that we have a service for your brother tonight and that your head might not be in the right place."

Mark held my gaze for a moment before nodding and letting go of my hand. "Fair enough."

"Fair enough?" Craig snarled. "You've got to be kidding me!" He turned his glare onto Aidan, tiny flares of gold spread through his eyes. "Haven't you taken enough from us? My dad, my brother, my girl. Now you want to take away the team, too."

"Craig, no one is taking anything away," I murmured. "We just ..."

"Save it, Jade," he growled. "Save your damn sympathy for someone who actually wants it."

Aidan's scent suddenly flared, and his fingers stopped their lazy trail on my neck. His body stiffened. I glanced up at him and opened my mouth, ready to tell him to chill out, but the words died on my tongue.

His eyes were starting to change. Little speckles of

gold dotted the soft brown. But he wasn't looking at Craig. He was staring at the entrance of the diner. His face was rock hard, his jaw clenching and unclenching. He moved in his seat slightly, his chest pressing against my shoulder, and I felt the vibration of his soft growl before I heard it.

He nudged me and jerked his chin, signaling me to let him out of the booth. The guys were already standing, their focus fixed on the doors as they swung open.

CHAPTER 9

AIDAN

"What's wrong with you guys?" Jade asked. She was looking at the team and me as if we'd all lost our minds. "Sit down. You're going to make a ..." Her voice trailed off as she sucked in a long, slow breath. Her upper lip started to curl up into a snarl, and her gaze snapped to the door as it banged shut.

"Let me out, sweetheart," I said roughly. I didn't want to push her out of the way, but damn, I would if I had to. I wasn't going to let them anywhere near her. My inner-wolf clawed at my chest, anxious and unnerved. Low growls erupted from the guys as they started to move from our table toward the door.

"You're not going anywhere," she hissed, pushing against my chest. "Sit down, guys." She didn't take the chance that they wouldn't listen to her and used the full force of her new scent to bring their focus back to her. When she had their full attention, she placed her hands on the table, fingers splayed wide, and said, "Sit." Her tone was all command.

The guys didn't waste a second in obeying her. They slid back into the booth quickly, taking their seats, but their gazes never left the doorway.

No one in the restaurant seemed to notice the soft growls that rumbled around our table. Utensils continued to clank against plates. Mugs slapped against tables. People chatted. Just like any other morning at the diner. They didn't have a clue about the threat.

I glanced back at the entrance. The two men had stopped just inside the doorway. Both of them were in their late thirties, cleanly shaven, and dressed in jeans and bright orange hunting jackets. One was tall, gangly looking, and the other, shorter and stubby. Their gazes drifted over the busy restaurant before coming to a rest at our table.

The tall one pulled out a cell phone, thumbed the screen, and brought it to his ear. He kept his eyes on us the entire time. His lips moved, but I couldn't make out anything other than the vague tone of his voice over the clatter from the other patrons.

The call didn't even last a minute, and he shoved his phone back into his pocket. The waitress appeared in front of them, menus in her hand, but they waved her away and took up a post just inside the doors as if they were waiting for friends to show before grabbing a table. And I figured that's exactly what they were doing. Waiting for friends.

"Jade," I said sternly, shifting in the bench seat to face her. "This place is packed. We have to ..."

Jade cut me off. "Aidan, there are only two of them." She waved a hand in their direction. "Not really what I'd call threatening. Even if that phone call he just made was for back-up, the guys could handle it." She huffed out a breath through her nose and folded her arms over her chest. "And we're in public. You can't go all wolfy and attack them here in the diner. People might be used to seeing wolves around town, but they never see the violence. You'll just freak everyone out."

I let out a frustrated growl, and she gave me the eyebrow. It was just one, lifting on the right, and matched with the look in her eyes, it clearly said, *I dare you to argue. You know I'm right.*

Jade, the freakin' voice of reason. When the hell did that happen? She was more of an act first type, and besides that, she'd also been an emotional mess all morning, yelling at me one second and close to tears the next. But now, there wasn't a single trace of nerves in her scent. She was focused. She was thinking. And she was completely in command.

Her gaze swept over the room before returning back to me. "Stop looking at me like I've grown another head," she said with a little laugh, placing a hand on my cheek. "You knew damn well they'd try again after last night. You even told me so this morning."

"Exactly," I said. I was losing patience, so was my inner-wolf. My skin felt as if it were crawling. Coarse hair darkened my forearms, and I was certain my eyes were a nice shade of gold. "Which is exactly why you need to move that cute butt of yours before I move it for you, sweetheart."

I glanced back at the entrance. The men still hadn't moved. They were leaning against the wall to the side of the doorway, with their gazes locked on our table. Waiting.

"What happened last night?" Landon asked. He sounded concerned, but his scent screamed guilt.

I leaned forward, rested my forearms on the table, and glared at him. "If you'd bothered to answer your phone, you wouldn't have to ask."

The others shifted uncomfortably in their seats, making clear efforts not to glance at Jade or me. But Landon ... he was going to argue with me. I could see it. He even muttered something, but his words were lost in a growl that ripped from his throat.

Jade smacked her hands on the table. "Enough," she said, quietly yet fiercely. She waited for a second, making sure we were listening, and then with certainty, she said, "They'll come to us."

"What are they waiting for?" Beck asked.

"I'm guessing they're waiting for more to show." She pulled out her cell phone and started tapping out a message. Seconds after she sent it, her phone chirped with a response. She smiled, looking extremely proud of herself, and she glanced up. "At least half the pack will be outside in five minutes. The rest won't be far behind, so chill out. We will not cause a scene in front of this many people if we don't have to. It wouldn't be good for our image." Her smile faded, and she glared at me then, long and hard, before shifting that glare around the table. "We'll finish our discussion later. Got it?"

The guys nodded and mumbled what sounded like an agreement. It never failed to shock me how quickly the team responded to her orders. It confused me, amazed me, and troubled me all at once. But then, most things to do with Jade left me feeling like that.

"Who'd you message?" I asked, wrapping my arm around her shoulder, attempting to look calm, but I wasn't sure if I succeeded. My inner-wolf was going crazy within me. He wanted to defend our territory. He wanted to protect our mate. He wanted blood. And sitting here doing nothing was putting him (and me) on edge.

Her response was an eye roll as if the answer was obvious, and she said, "Dom."

Jade had been right. The cougars came to us. It took another three minutes for the men to finally push off the wall and make their way over to our table. It seemed to take forever for them to reach us. They moved slowly, with a cocky self-confidence that seemed out of place since it was just the two of them, and there were six of us.

"You've got a good step up out there," the tall one said with a sly smile when he reached us. "Good, but not great. It only took about an hour to slip through your patrols."

"Wait until you try to get back out," Mark drawled with a lazy grin. He lifted his mug and took a sip.

"Don't see that being much of a problem," the short one said. He grabbed a chair, spun it around, and straddled it, resting his arms on the top of the backrest.

I growled. Their scent so close made my skin crawl, and it took everything in me to sit still and keep my arm around Jade. My inner-wolf was jerking against my skin. That guy really needed to stop eyeing Jade's cleavage, or he was going to find himself dead shortly. She was barely showing any skin, dressed in jeans, her plum zip-up hoodie, which was open with a form-fitting black tee underneath. The neckline scooped barely below the crease of her breasts, but the way he was looking at her chest, it was as if she had nothing on.

Jade wiggled against me, and I felt the shudder of her skin as she pressed her back to my chest, facing them. She pushed her palm against my knee as another growl bounced around my chest, and she snapped the fingers on her other hand, drawing the man's attention away from her chest.

"What can we help you with?" she asked sweetly as if she was genuinely interested, but she didn't quite manage to hide the growled roughness of her inner-wolf in her tone.

"You're Jade, right?" the tall one asked from his spot behind the jackass in the chair, arms folded. "Jeff's daughter?"

"That's me," she answered with another sweet as sugar smile.

The one in the chair let his eyes drop to her chest again, and my inner-wolf pressed against my ribs. "Do it again," I snarled. "Check out her chest again, and I swear, you'll be dead before you can suck in one more breath."

"Aidan, baby, chill," Jade said, looking over at me. Her eyes were screaming at me to rein it in, but her tone was still sugar-sweet.

The team watched her curiously, and by their soft chuckles, I thought they were probably getting a kick out of her sweetness, which we all knew was a joke. It wasn't that Jade wasn't sweet. She could be — sometimes — but I thought the fluttery eyelashes were pushing it a little.

I smirked at her, forcing my inner-wolf back. "Jade, sweetheart, I'm completely chilled."

I knew what she was trying to do with her sweet and innocent act. She was buying us time for the pack to show. It was probably smart. No. It was definitely smart. There were too many people here. Too many witnesses to drag them out back and beat the shit out of them like I wanted. Doing something like that would probably ruin the werewolf/human relationship in Dog Mountain.

There was a beat of silence, and then the chubby one in the chair said, "Your dad's pretty worried about you. He sent us to bring you back home."

I laughed at that. So did the guys. But Jade didn't. She gave him a look that was a little sad and a lot concerned. "What did you do to get on my dad's bad side?"

The tall one shook his head in confusion. "Not on his bad side."

"Really?" she said. "It seems to me you have to be."

She sighed, and her frown deepened. "I just can't think of any other reason why he'd send you guys in here while I'm with my mate having a meeting with our pack enforcers."

JADE

I almost felt bad for the two men in front of me. Almost. They glanced at the guys, their faces turning a sickly shade of gray. Obviously, my father hadn't bothered to tell them who I'd most likely be with when they tracked me down. It made me hate him even more. I knew he didn't have much concern for human life, but really, did he not even care about his own pack?

I opened my mouth to tell them as much but was stopped short by a high-pitched shout. "Get out of my way, Dominic!" My heart tripped at the panicked voice. Mom. There goes not causing a scene. I swiveled in my seat and winced, catching sight of her pushing and shoving at Dominic's chest, trying and failing to get past him. "I'm serious," she shouted. "Get out of my way!"

I glanced back at the werecougars, taking in their smug grins. Every cell in my body buzzed with awareness. These two weren't here to bring me back to my father. They were only here to track me down. I was sure that my dad knew they'd never stand a chance, just the two of them. And I was also pretty sure that he didn't expect to see them again. They hadn't been calling in reinforcements. They'd been calling for my mother.

I had to admit that it was actually a pretty smart play, sending in someone I loved who couldn't defend themselves against a bunch of shifters. Dad knew I wouldn't ignore her. That I'd protect her. That I'd leave with her to get her out of harm's way.

The tall one chuckled, and I shot him a dirty look. He shrugged. "Like I said, we're not on his bad side. Your mom's pretty worried, too. She wasn't too happy to hear about how your mate manhandled you and tossed you into a car." His expression changed to one of mock concern. "If he does that in public, one can only wonder what kind of a beating he gave you when he got you back home."

I laughed once, feeling sick and cold and a little shaky. "Dom!" I called, drawing his attention. People were starting to look. At us. At Mom and Dominic.

I waved him over. Mom stopped flailing and yelling, and she stepped around him. She rushed toward us with a determined gait. She'd dressed in a hurry. I couldn't remember ever seeing her leave the house in jogging pants before. Her face was splotchy and tear-stained. Her hair was a tangled mess.

I needed to think. If Dominic was here, most of the pack would be with him. I took a quick look out the large front window, spotting the two wolves and a few other pack members in human form pacing the parking lot. People walked by the wolves, barely paying them any attention, as if seeing them in town was a normal occurrence, but then, I guessed it kind of was normal. It should have made me feel better, but at that moment, it really didn't.

When Mom reached our table, Aidan let his arm drop from my shoulder, and he sat a little straighter beside me. "Hi, Pam," he said casually, if not a bit cautiously. He offered her a smile, which actually looked pretty believable, but it didn't fool me. His scent carried a hot spike of anger.

Mom completely ignored him, keeping her tear-filled eyes on me. "Jade, honey. You need to come with me right now." She held out a hand to me, her eyes pleading with me to take it.

I hesitated. I didn't know what to do. She couldn't stay here, and I wasn't going to leave with her and go to my dad. I didn't know what lies she'd been told, but by the way she was glaring at Aidan, I could take a pretty good guess.

"Pam, why don't you sit down for a minute?" Beck said, waving to the empty place beside me.

Mom dropped her outstretched hand. She glanced at Beck and then at the others as if she were only noticing them now. Her face crumbled, and she made a strangled sound from the back of her throat. "I trusted you boys," she whispered. "How could you let this happen to her?"

Resolve settled itself in my belly as I listened to my mom and saw the heartbreak in her eyes. It was time. She needed to know everything. Beck opened his mouth, but I jumped in before he could get anything out. "Aidan, give me your keys."

The werecougar who'd sat down rose from his chair and said, "You're not going anywhere." He folded his arms over his chest. I thought he was probably trying to go for tough, but he failed. He was short, stubby; he might be a shifter, but he clearly wasn't a match for the team or Aidan.

I laughed once, a startling sound, and slid out of the booth. "You really think you can stop me? Look around this table." My voice was rising, coated with anger, and I waved a hand toward the front window. "Look outside."

The men looked to where I pointed, and they cursed under their breath. They started to back away but didn't make it far. Landon and Mark were out of their seats in a blink, blocking their way.

I looked down at Aidan, still sitting in the booth.

He hadn't moved to grab his keys. He gave me a look that said he wasn't letting me out of his sight. "I need a pedicure," I said and held out my hand to Aidan.

"Shit," Dominic muttered from his place behind my mom. "Jade, maybe that's not ..."

I cut him a look and didn't let him finish. "It's time, Dom. Call Mac, okay?" I looked back to Aidan and held his eyes, pleading with him not to argue. "Give me your keys," I demanded. "I'm taking Mom back to our place."

He frowned. I knew he was confused. I knew he had no idea what I was doing or thinking. He glanced at Dominic, then at my mom, and then he dug his keys out of his pocket and tossed them to me. "Take Mark and a couple other members with you."

I leaned into him, kissing the corner of his mouth. "Love you, baby."

CHAPTER 10

AIDAN

Jade needed a pedicure.

Not very long ago, I thought that having Jade in my life would never be boring. I wasn't wrong. Since meeting her, I hadn't had a boring day. I hadn't even had a boring hour. I remembered being happy about that, knowing that no two days would ever be the same. I was glad that she didn't back down with me. She challenged me. She surprised me. She kept me on my toes.

Now, though, a part of me wanted the boring. We had two werecougars at our table. We still hadn't come to a decision on what to do with the team. Her mom thought I was abusing her. Her dad was clearly done pretending to be working with us. The werecougars were not only trying to bring in more women but there were three kids, one of them, a young girl within their clutches. And Jade thought now was the time for a freakin' pedicure. I seriously didn't even know what to think about that.

Jade wrapped an arm around her mother's waist and ushered her through the diner, Mark following closely behind her. She didn't look back, not once, and in a few short seconds, she was out the door.

Letting her go went against every protective instinct I had. I wasn't the only one struggling with it either. The team, Dominic, we were all on edge. But that determined glint in her eyes ... I knew if I didn't give her the keys, she would have left anyway. Having the car with locked doors made me feel a bit better, but not much.

I met Dominic's eyes and arched an eyebrow when the door shut behind them. He knew I wanted to know what this *pedicure* crap was about, but he only shook his head. He looked conflicted, as if he weren't entirely sure if he should stop her or let her go. It was obvious that he knew exactly what Jade was up to. He huffed and shook his head again, and then he yanked out his phone, most likely to call Marcy.

"I'm still thinking that these morons pissed off Jeff," Craig said. He rose slowly and stretched his arms over his head lazily.

"Yep," I agreed. "Or he just forgot to give them an exit strategy." I lifted my shoulders in a half-hearted shrug. "Maybe it's just a simple oversight."

I looked at our guests. I didn't have a clue what to do with them. I couldn't just let them go. Except right then, that's exactly what I wanted to do. If only to give me the time to go after Jade and find out what the hell she was up to.

"You all aren't going to do anything," the chubby one sneered. "We're in public."

"We're in a town that loves our pack," Beck said. He was smiling, a manic kind of smile that actually gave me a little chill. He jerked his chin toward the front of the diner, pointing out the wolves still pacing in the parking lot. "No one even blinks at our presence."

The waitress started our way, a couple menus

clutched against her chest. Her bright smile was gone, a forced one in its place. She stopped at our table. "Menus?" she asked, looking at our company and then back to me. Her scent told me she was a bit nervous, but she was far from scared. I couldn't really blame her, not after watching Pam's little freak out with Dominic at the door.

"They won't be staying," I said, smiling as warmly as I could. "And we won't be either. Could you put a stop on our order?"

She nodded, and her face fell, disappointed. "Sure."

I pulled out my wallet and tossed a few twenties on the table to cover our bill before standing up. I waved my hand in an *after-you* kind of gesture to our guests and said, "Let's go."

The guys moved in around the werecougars, forcing them to walk through the utterly quiet diner. People watched us move, although it wasn't with fear. It was curious gazes that followed us out, and I found myself thinking that it was actually kind of nice that the town knew about us, trusted us. It sure made some parts of pack life a hell of a lot easier.

The werecougars didn't put up a fight. No. They moved out the doors without a word, heads hanging. I thought they were probably clued into the fact that no one was coming to help them. That Jeff had thrown them to the wolves — literally. At least these two had some sense of self-preservation, unlike the idiot who'd bitten me last night. Or maybe they had just simply given up. The truth? I didn't really care either way.

There were more pack members in wolf form than I'd noticed from inside in the parking lot. Six wolves, all various shades of brown, circled Beck, Craig, and Landon, as they put the cougars into a truck and got in. A couple of the pack members hopped into the truck bed, and then they pulled out of the lot. The wolves loped after them, and I gave out orders for everyone else to head back to the headquarters.

I rode back to the headquarters with Dominic. It was a fairly silent drive, but not entirely. He huffed a lot and clicked his tongue. It was as if he wanted to talk, but he couldn't find the words when he tried. It was weird. Crazy weird. Dominic always had something to say, and he never held back. He looked defeated, I thought, and it made my skin crawl with a bizarre mix of dread and anticipation. "You want to tell me what this pedicure stuff is all about?" I asked.

Dominic chuckled softly and cut me a quick sideways look. "You don't know that girl at all, do you?"

"Sure I do," I said quickly, except it didn't sound believable. "She's mine. Of course, I know her."

From the quick look Dominic gave me, I knew he hadn't expected to hear anything else, and after a few long beats, he muttered, "Pedicure is code for *I'm freaking out and need girl time.*"

"Girl time," I repeated and blinked. "You're kidding me."

"I'm dead serious, Aidan," Dominic said. "Hard conversations take place during *girl time*. They won't answer phones or let anyone in that house until everything that needs to be said is said."

Dominic made a left. Up ahead, I spotted the truck carrying the werecougars as it turned into the headquarters' parking lot. I figured I could lock them up for a bit, but it was only a temporary fix, and I wasn't even sure if keeping them here was a good idea. We had two dead from last night at the building. And now another two alive. I was pretty sure they'd pick up the scent of the dead fairly quickly. Maybe they'd go ballistic when they did, and the pack would solve the *what to do with them* problem quickly?

I scrubbed at my face roughly. Yep, I seriously needed some *boring* when this was over.

"She's going to tell Pam everything." It wasn't a question. I'd seen the determination in her eyes before she left. I'd thought she'd been determined to get her mother away from the enemy. But this ... My lips tugged up at the corners. This was better. "Jade's done protecting her father."

Dominic grunted, "Yep."

More huff-filled silence as he pulled into the parking lot and found a spot. I knew he had something else to say, and for the life of me, I didn't have a clue why he was holding it back. He never had before, and when the next long huff puffed out of him, I snapped, "Just spit it out, Dom."

"Just thinking that this crap with the team needs to end," he said, turning off the car. "You need them. Jade needs them. Hell, the pack might hate them most of the time, but they need those guys, too." I cut him a look, and his hands quickly shot up. He continued with caution. "I'm not saying that we should just forget what they did, but you can't blame them for wanting to help their brother. Not unless you're going to start blaming Jade for stalling with her dad. If you stop and really think about it, they were doing the same thing she's been doing. And don't tell me you haven't let her stall things because we all know you have."

He was not wrong. He knew it. I knew it. I was sure the whole damn pack knew it, too. I knew I didn't look happy when I asked, "What am I supposed to do? I can't just let what they did go. She could have gotten hurt. I could have lost her."

I didn't expect an answer, and I was sure Dominic knew that, but he decided to give me one anyway, and his answer sucked. "Don't really know what you're supposed to do. But you didn't lose her, Aidan. She's fine. And those guys let their brother die to keep her and our pack safe."

I nodded because I really didn't know what to say, and we got out of the car. Groups of pack members huddled around the entrance, watching the team pull our guests out of the truck, and it was at that moment, as I scanned the clusters of people, that I realized Tommy and Chris hadn't shown up yet.

"You see Tommy and Chris today?" I asked as I shut my door.

Dominic glanced over the car with his typical cool mask tightly back in place. "Yeah, sorry. I forgot to tell you. Your dad called them. They're going to be tied up for a few hours."

JADE

It was only 9:17 in the morning, and my day had already turned to crap.

Marcy was standing at the table, noisily sorting through a bag of nail polish that, thankfully, Dominic had told her to bring. She'd been waiting on the front deck with Trevor when Mom and I drove up. I hadn't had to explain what I was about to do. The look she'd given me told me she already knew. I wasn't sure exactly how, but I thought that was probably Dominic's doing as well.

Mom sat in a chair at the kitchen table, her feet submerged in the footbath. She was in a state. She looked dazed and vulnerable and sad. She muttered a lot. Mostly about how sorry she was for pushing me toward the pack — toward Aidan.

"Mom, Aidan would never hit me." It was just a whisper from me, but it was full of sincerity. "And if he tried, he'd be dead. You know the team wouldn't allow it."

I wasn't sure if that was entirely true, but it sounded good. The team loved me. I knew they did, but Aidan was their alpha male, and I was his mate. In the eyes of the pack, Aidan could do pretty much whatever he wanted with me. I was basically his property. But it worked both ways. He was also mine. They probably wouldn't stop me from beating the crap out of him either if I wanted to, which, of course, I didn't.

She didn't believe me. I could see it, feel it, God, I could even smell it. "Ray ..."

"Aidan. Is. Not. Ray." I said it with clear precision, biting each word clean off, with sharp edges and all.

Mom screamed, a short burst of sound that made both Marcy and me jump. It was pure rage and frustration, boiling out of her. Her body shuddered. Her fists clenched. I'd never seen her like this. Never. "Why would your father tell me this if he didn't watch it happen, Jade?"

Mark burst into the kitchen, his breath panting and his eyes focused, searching for a threat. He opened his mouth, most likely to demand what was going on, and I gestured to him, an indication for him not to speak. He frowned, confused, but shut his mouth and propped himself against the doorframe.

My heart was aching, and I pulled in a quick, shaky breath. "I think the better question is why would Dad let me leave with Aidan if he saw that happening to me?"

Mom's eyes widened, and she made a strangled whimpering sound, but she didn't answer my question.

"You know what Mr. Shaw is, Mom," Marcy said. She sounded calm and gentle, and she moved to kneel beside my mom, looking up at her with big, sad eyes. "Don't you?"

Mom nodded. She didn't make a sound. Her gaze was locked on Marcy, waiting breathlessly for some kind of explanation — a link — to make what she thought she knew make sense. And I had that link.

The video.

"Then you know that he could have stepped in easily," Marcy continued delicately. "If Aidan had really punched her in the face like you were told, Mr. Shaw could have stopped it."

I felt myself smile. I had no idea why, because well, this wasn't really a smiling moment, and by no means did I feel happy. But then, maybe the smile was coming from relief. I was going to tell Mom everything. Right now. I wasn't going to have to lie to her anymore.

"Mark," I said. My voice was a little shaky, but I still managed to hold onto that smile. "Can you go upstairs and grab Aidan's laptop? It should be on the dresser in our bedroom."

He nodded to me just a little, and his smile was one of approval and encouragement as he turned and headed for the stairs.

When I looked back at Mom, her face had changed. It went from grief-stricken and enraged to something so twisted with an uncertainty that it made my heartbeat quicken painfully fast. I pulled out a chair and took a seat beside her, clasping her hand in my own. "Mom, there's something I need you to see."

CHAPTER 11

AIDAN

"We should be doing something," Landon said, pacing the floor. We were back in my office with Craig, Beck, and Dominic, trying to figure out the best move, except we weren't getting far. "We should be getting those kids or killing those bastards. We should not be giving them a comfy room and wasting our resources guarding them."

Landon had a point, but unfortunately, the cougars hadn't put up any kind of a fight. The two men were completely and totally compliant as they were led through the headquarters. They kept their mouths shut, and their gazes dropped. I thought they probably knew there was no point in fighting. We outnumbered them too greatly for them to even consider that they might have had a chance at getting away.

Now they were locked up in one of the old bedrooms at the back of the building with four pack members guarding the door. It was a complete waste of man-power, but right then, I really didn't know what else to do with them, and there was just something so ... wrong about killing two men who were showing their submission, even if they did deserve death for the things they'd done with their pack.

"We can't just rush out there," Beck said. He was sitting on the couch, one arm strewn over the back and legs stretched out in front of him. "That's how people get hurt. We need a plan, and yelling about how we should be doing something is not helping."

"We should kill them now!" Craig shouted, from his spot beside Beck, causing Beck to groan and roll his eyes. He wasn't alone with the eye roll.

Craig was twitchy, and his neck had a splash of color slowly creeping up to his face. He was looking at Beck as if he were ready to pummel him for attempting to be reasonable. His fists, clenched and white-knuckled. His jaw flexed so tight the muscles looked as if they were beating under his skin.

"They could be useful," I said from where I leaned against the wall, arms folded across my chest. "We need to consider that before getting rid of them."

Craig moved, jumping up from the couch and crossing the room with speed, and before I could say anything more, he was standing in front of me. The color had reached his cheeks, a bright red. His eyes flared, and he shouted, "They were after your mate, our alpha female. They would have taken her if we hadn't been there."

My eyes narrowed at the thought, and ignoring Craig's outburst, I pushed off the wall, stepped around him, and joined in on Landon's useless pacing. It was true. They had been after her, and if Jade had been alone, they probably would have taken her, although not without one hell of a fight, I was sure.

"But you guys were there, and they didn't take her," Dominic pointed out, drawing all of our gazes. He sat on top of my desk, his hands on his thighs, leaning forward slightly. "No point in fighting over what could have happened."

Dominic fixed me with a look that I tried really hard to ignore as a round of grunted agreement filtered through the guys.

And then there was silence. It was thoughtful and a little tense, and it stretched on longer than any silence really should.

Craig went back to the couch, taking a hard seat. Landon started to pace again, six steps across the room, six steps back. Beck scrubbed at his face, the frown lines deepening.

It struck me then, as I watched them, that these guys were probably more dedicated to the pack than any other member we had. Even now, not knowing whether or not they would still be enforcers tomorrow, they were here, ready to fight. Giving me guidance. And I couldn't ignore that they'd had my back in the diner even after I'd made it clear that I didn't trust them and didn't want them on the team.

Maybe Dominic was on to something. There really wasn't any point in arguing about the *could haves*. When I actually thought about it, most of my anger toward the guys was based on the *could haves*. I could have lost Jade. Jared could have taken the pack from me. The team could have stood by and not said anything about the cougars' location. They could have given Jared more time. They could have taken over his quest for revenge.

But they didn't. None of that happened. I still had Jade and the pack. Jared was gone, and the team was still here, backing me.

The truth? I was starting to think that I'd let my emotions where Jade was concerned run my decisions when it came to these guys, and damn, it made me feel guilty.

"Jade was right," I said, breaking the silence. I went back to my post, leaning against the wall. "I was harsh this morning."

"Don't worry," Beck said, brushing it off with a shrug. "We get it. Emotions are running high all around." He gave me a meaningful look, one that was full of understanding and didn't hold any trace of malice, and for reasons I really didn't want to explore, I found myself looking away. "Aidan, you've got to stop blaming yourself because no one else does."

"He's right," Craig said, still angry. "You made the right call with our dad, and you made it again with Jared." He pulled in a breath and let it out. "But I'm telling you, taking this team apart is not the right call."

"I know." It was all I could say. Tension that I didn't even realize was there eased from my shoulders. Deep down, I thought I'd known that all along.

"Awesome." Landon's voice oozed sarcasm. "Now that we have the obvious out of the way, can someone tell me why Jeff would kick Jade out if he was going to drag her back anyway?" He looked utterly confused. "What was the point?"

What was the point of any of this? If there was one, I couldn't see it. It just didn't make sense. Jeff didn't strike me as a stupid man. Hell, he'd had the pack fooled for years. If it wasn't for that video of him making a deal with Tiffany, we probably still wouldn't have known what this pack was doing. So why now? What was he hoping to gain from having Jade tucked back in his house?

"Aidan?" Dominic called.

I raised a hand. "Hold on." My thoughts started to race. I took a breath and held it as I tried to understand what I was even thinking. Everything was so jumbled. Flashes of the last couple of months. Partial conversation. They all swarmed in and mashed together until everything collided with sharp clarity. I blinked, looked at Dominic, and said, "He needed us mated."

"Why?" Landon asked with barely any patience.

"Because now that we're mated, she carries my scent," I said. "She doesn't need me to control the entire pack. If he can convince her to work with him, she can force everyone to accept it. Through her, he could run our pack."

"We need to get rid of him, Aidan," Dominic said. There was anger in the statement, but also there was resolution and maybe a little fear. "He needs to be taken out."

"No," I said sharply. "As far as we know, he's the only real authority those bastards have. If we take that, there's no one to keep them in line, no one for them to follow." But as I said it, I had only one clear, crisp thought: *We're going to take him and his pack down.*

JADE

"She took that better than I thought she would," Marcy whispered from beside me as we watched my mom dig through the fridge. The pedicures had been completely forgotten. She'd decided I had to be hungry since she'd interrupted my breakfast and was determined to make a meal.

"I think she's trying not to process it," I whispered back as Mom put a carton of eggs on the counter and kept rummaging through the fridge.

"Jade," Mom called. Her voice was chipper, almost sing-song. "Can you run to the store? We don't have enough eggs for pancakes. Oh, and maybe some more bacon."

"I think we should call Aidan," I said. "Get the guys

back here." Not that they would be able to help with this, but honestly, Mom was freaking me out a little. Her scent kept spiking with hot fear, and each time it did, she became a little more frantic, riffling through the fridge.

"Jade?" Mom pulled her head out and looked over her shoulder at me. Her smile was bright and brittle, and her eyes, utterly blank. "Why are you just standing there? Run to the store. Hurry up. We have a lot to do before Jared's service this evening." And with that, she stuck her head back into the fridge and said, "We need orange juice, too."

I heaved a sigh, watching as she pretty much emptied every piece of food that was somewhat breakfast-related onto the counter. Maybe I shouldn't have dumped everything on her all at once, but the thing was, once I'd started talking, I hadn't been able to stop. There was just something so lightening in getting it all out.

After letting her watch the video, I'd launched in, telling her all about the cougars. I explained how they only seemed to change males and locked up women in barbed wire cages. I told her about the kids they had and the *accident*, which left the cougars womanless, and I explained that Dad was their pack leader.

I went on to tell her all about Jared. About how he'd known where the cougars were and hidden it from us. I explained that once his brothers found out, they had turned him in, and then he'd challenged for alpha. Though, I might have left out the little part about my helping Aidan kill him. I couldn't say why exactly, but I thought it might have had something to do with the overwhelming guilt I was feeling over the whole situation. I couldn't help but think that if I hadn't been so consumed with hurting Aidan, I would have seen what Jared had been up to before it was too late.

And then I told her about last night and about the two dead cougars we now had at the headquarters. And finally, I explained that Aidan had only picked me up and tossed me into the car yesterday because I'd basically told Dad that I didn't trust him at all and accused him of protecting those monsters.

Marcy leaned into me and pressed her lips to my ear. "Maybe she's in denial."

"Yeah, maybe," I said, but I wasn't really sure if that was what this was. Actually, going by her scent, I thought she was pretty close to freaking out. This wasn't denial. It was Mom trying to be strong and cope.

A pot clattered to the floor, and Mom bent down to pick it up. She glanced back at us, the pot clutched tightly in her hands. "Go on, honey," she said. She smiled again, another breakable smile. "You're wasting time."

I tried to smile back, but whatever my lips did, it wasn't a smile, and because I really didn't know what else to say, I muttered, "Sure, Mom," as I snagged Marcy's hand and tugged her from the room.

The living room was surprisingly quiet, and it took me a moment to notice Mark sprawled out on the couch, with an arm thrown over his eyes.

Marcy went to the far end and plopped down, not caring that she jostled his feet, but then I thought he probably didn't care either because all he did was readjust, lifting them up and dropping them on her lap.

Marcy made a tragic face, looking at his feet in her lap and then up at him. She looked as if she were going to tell him to get up, but then she shook her head, pursed her lips, and looked at me. "Tell me you're not really going to the store."

"Ummm ..." I took a quick look over my shoulder,

seeing Mom rush about the kitchen, and fought back the feeling that I'd just made a really big mistake.

There was a sound, just on the edge of my hearing, and I glanced out the window. It sounded like voices, and at first, I thought it was just the two other pack members that had come with us from the diner. They'd stayed outside under Mark's orders to watch the house. But then it got louder, and there were more voices than just two.

There was a light knock at the door, and then it swung open. "Jade," Erika said with a little nod. She stepped into the house, five other women trailed in behind her. "We need to talk to you."

CHAPTER 12

AIDAN

The phone rang, and for a moment, I felt relieved that something was interrupting me from loading bodies into the bed of Jared's (or I guess it was now Beck's) truck, because really, who wanted to handle dead bodies? But we needed to get rid of them, and bringing them back to Jeff, just as Jade had suggested last night, seemed like a good plan. We were hoping that two more dead bodies to contend with would give us a little extra time to devise and execute a solid plan for extracting the children. According to the team's report, the kids weren't in any immediate danger, but I didn't want to risk waiting. Instead of being manipulative, Jeff was becoming aggressive, and we needed to get those kids out before we retaliated with our own attack. It was safer that way. Fewer distractions. Fewer innocent that could get hurt.

When I dug my phone out of my pocket, my first thought was that it was Jade. Maybe she'd finished up with her mother, and she was calling to see where I was. My second thought was that it could be Tommy or Chris. I'd left them each messages, trying to get a feel on if or when they'd be coming back. You just never knew with my dad. It wouldn't surprise me at all that he'd decide to take them back before I was ready to let them go. He was the master of reneging on a gift.

I cradled my phone in my palm, about to thumb the screen when I read the caller display: *Unknown.* I stared at it for a moment, hesitated, frowned. I usually let unknown calls go to voicemail, and right now, I really didn't have time to politely dismiss a telemarketer. Still, then with everything going on, I didn't want to miss something important, so, curious, I answered, "Hello?"

My greeting was answered by a frustrated sounding groan, and then a familiar and anxious voice said, "Where's Jade?"

I laughed once — stunned. After last night and this morning, I really hadn't expected this call. I thought more along the lines of cougars coming into town trying to fight their way to her. Not an anxious phone call. "If you were looking for Jade, you probably should have called her phone."

"That's who I was calling." Jeff sounded strained, and it was then that I realized that I never removed the call forwarding from Jade's phone last night. All her calls were still being routed to me.

I moved away from the truck and the guys and headed for the back of the building where the picnic table was. I probably shouldn't have. It couldn't have looked good on my part. I was sure they had picked up the unease in my scent when I heard his voice. Still, I guess not trusting the team had become sort of a habit in the last little while, and before I really realized I was doing it, I was sitting on top of the table, listening to Jeff's breathing on the other end of the line.

I waited for a beat for him to tell me what the hell he wanted, but he didn't. Just more heavy breathing. With a huff, I asked, "What do you want, Jeff?"

There was a catch in Jeff's voice. "I-I wanted to talk to my daughter and my wife."

For a moment, I was silent. He sounded ... desperate? "Well, we don't always get what we want, do we?" I kept my tone casual, which took a crazy amount of effort. "You're getting sloppy, Jeff, and sloppiness, well, that's a sign of desperation. Honestly, I figured you'd be more worried about what we were doing with the two cougars you sent to get her this morning."

"I didn't ..."

"Really?" I blurted, cutting him off. "Are you really going to try to tell me you didn't send them? And I bet you're going to deny filling Pam's head full of lies about me beating up Jade, too."

"I want my daughter home." Jeff's voice shook, and I couldn't tell if it was from anger or nerves. "Give her back, and I'll make sure you never see or hear from the cougars again."

"Is that the deal you were telling Luken about?" I bit out the question sharply and didn't wait for him to answer before I spat, "I'm not scared to fight for what I want, and I will fight for it. For her. For this pack. For this town."

I heard a breath and then utter silence. I pulled the phone away from my ear and glanced at the screen. He hung up. I gazed at it blankly for a moment. Desperate. He was desperate. I was sure of that. But then, if I had four pack members go missing in less than twenty-four hours, I'd probably be desperate, too.

What did that leave them with? The team had come back with a count of twenty, although they hadn't been able to get close enough to be certain of that number. Even so, if we went with that number, it meant that the cougars were down to sixteen, seventeen including Jeff, which, I realized, put his pack back at the exact number that he'd given us to start with.

I wondered if those four had always been expendable. Had he figured he'd lose them all along, or was it just a lucky chance for us?

"Who was that?" Beck asked from behind me.

I pushed my hair back and looked over my shoulder. "Jeff."

Beck rounded the table and hopped up beside me. I could feel his eyes on me, watching, waiting. "In the diner, you said blunt and open," he reminded me after a few beats of silence. He looked very serious, I noticed, as I glanced over at him. "You told Jade it was better that way. Don't you think it's time to use that logic?"

I set my phone down slowly. "Beck ..."

"No," he said, raising up his hands as if they would ward off what I was going to say. "I don't want to hear it. I can't take any more excuses. Ray might have been an asshole, and yeah, I'm glad he's gone, but at least when he ran this pack, everything was out in the open."

"Not everything," I countered. "None of you knew anything about this little deal with Jeff."

"Right." His nostrils flared, and his gaze hardened. "Do you trust me?"

Did I? For the most part, I thought I did, at least to a certain extent. Jade trusted him. Hell, she trusted all of them, and I knew she'd follow them blindly if they asked her to. But even if we'd just sort of cleared the air between us, and even if I thought I could trust him, there was still that small niggling voice chanting in the back of my head. *You killed his father and his brother.*

I sighed. "Beck, I don't think ..."

"I know exactly what you think," he growled. "You think that we're not going to be there when you need us. You think that if you tell us too much, we'll find your weakness and use it against you, just like Jared did. Well, newsflash, Aidan, we all know your weakness, so it's a little too late to try and keep that card close."

And Jade wondered why love should have nothing to do with the alpha pair. It wasn't something I liked to think about, not since I found her and especially not since I claimed her. Besides, it wasn't as if I'd ever want to go back and change what had happened between us. But at times, like this one, it was a struggle to look at everything and see what was best for the pack, not just what was best for her.

I nodded very slowly. "You're right. Everyone knows my weakness. It's not really a secret. But what most don't get is that she's also what keeps me strong. She's what keeps me fighting. I've killed for her, and I'll do it again. In a heartbeat."

"Good." The word was clipped, but his voice was softer when he continued. "Look, you're our alpha. The team and I will follow you, whether you want us to or not. I know you probably won't believe this, but we're glad it's you we're following. No one wanted to follow Ray. The pack, even us, we did it because we didn't have a choice. You and Jade ... you guys, have turned that around. People actually want to follow you." He smiled, chuckled, and shook his head as if the thought was a foreign one. "That's something, Aidan. You didn't know them before. Before, they were just scared. Scared of Ray. Scared of us. You've changed that. You've created a pack based on respect and compassion. Do you have any idea how refreshing it is to see pack members get second chances? I should be dead right now."

I shook my head. "You're alive because of Jade, not me."

Beck shrugged. "Yeah, maybe, but you agreed with her."

"Yes," I said. "Yes, I did." And I was really glad I'd agreed with her.

I looked down at my phone and tapped the screen. 9:42. I considered the phone call with Jeff, mostly because I didn't know what to say about everything Beck had just unloaded. I'd made it clear to Jeff exactly where I stood, and I figured the clock was probably now ticking on the cougars' current location. I wondered if he'd put that piece together yet. Did he realize that we knew where they were hiding? I thought that it could explain why he was taking risks that exposed him outright for what he really was, but still, I hoped that he didn't. We needed to get in and get those kids, fast, before we lost them again.

An idea then struck me, and I glanced up at Beck. "Change of plans. We're not bringing the dead back to Jeff, but I've got an idea on what to do with them."

Beck didn't say anything. He was probably waiting for me to tell him more, and for a moment, I couldn't find the words. My brain was too jumbled, weeding through the new opportunity, trying to find the flaws and the risks, mapping out the details.

When I finally got it out, I'd expected Beck to have an objection because my idea was rocky at best. But he didn't object. He actually seemed excited about the new plan, which was a serious relief, and when I finished, he'd gone back to fill in the rest of the team, leaving me at the picnic table with my cellphone in hand. I needed to know if I'd have Tommy and Chris for this, and there was really only one person that could tell me that.

So I made the call, even though I seriously didn't want to.

"Aidan." His voice was as harsh as a whip slapping against my skin. "Not a good time, son."

"Never is with you, Dad," I said, my phone jammed in between my shoulder and ear as I climbed off the table and started to pace. "But you're going to make time for this call."

He made a noncommittal kind of noise that I knew meant *perhaps*. It was the noise he always made when I demanded his time just before he blew me off.

I sighed. "You'll make time, Dad, or I'll get Mom involved. I'm sure she'd be interested to hear that you called Tommy and Chris away this morning."

"What do you need?" he said, rushed. "Make it quick." He sounded mildly annoyed at me, most likely for pulling the Mom card, but I didn't really care. It worked, and that was all that mattered.

"Tommy and Chris back would be nice," I said, and I maneuvered the phone from its place on my shoulder to my other ear. "If I remember your note correctly, it said they were mine until I was ready to give them back."

"I didn't need them here when I wrote the note," he said. "That changed yesterday."

I stopped pacing and jammed a hand into my pocket. "So you weren't even going to tell me?"

"Obviously, I didn't need to tell you, did I?"

"I thought you actually wanted me to succeed here."

"I do want you to succeed."

"Why'd you pull them out then?" I asked, trying to keep the emotion from my tone. It wasn't working. I could hear the hurt and the anger in my voice, and I was sure he could hear it, too. "You know damn well what I'm facing here, and you know I need them."

"Because," he said, "you're not the only one with problems. I've got a couple rogue wolves here that need dealing with."

"You've got to be shitting me," I blurted. "You called them away to deal with a couple rogues?"

"Pack before blood," he said. "It's always been that way. Always will be. It's not personal."

"Pack before blood," I echoed. I closed my eyes because I felt his words slice through me, and even a deep breath didn't set me right. How many times had he told me that? I couldn't even begin to count. It was pack before blood at my graduation. Pack before blood when my aunt — his sister — died. He hadn't shown at the funeral or my graduation because it was always pack before blood with him. Always. The thing was, the pack hadn't needed him then, but my mom and me, we'd needed him.

It was true. The pack was important, and in the end, I'd always pick what was best for the pack, just like the team had when it came to Jared. Except with my dad, he chose pack even when they didn't need him. And he always would. It was his escape from uncomfortable situations.

"That's never going to change, son," he said. There was a beat of silence, and when he spoke again, his tone was even harsher. "When Tommy shows up there, have him escorted back to me. My enforcers need a word with him."

"What are you talking about?" I asked and started to pace again. "What the hell did he do?"

"He refused to come home," Dad said coolly. "Dropped Chris off at a gas station, said he was done. He turned his back on his pack when he was needed and defied a direct order from me."

"So you're saying he refused to leave me to help you deal with your stupid rogues, and you want to kill him for it."

"That's what I'm saying."

I laughed once. He meant it, and it left me wordless

and stunned. Twenty years of service and my father was going to have Tommy killed because he'd decided to help me. There was no way I'd turn my back on him. Not when he was in shit because of me.

There was really only one thing to do, and that was to lay claim before my father could carry out his asinine execution plans, even if the idea of adding Tommy to my pack wasn't one that gave me a warm fuzzy feeling. "Good thing you're not his alpha anymore," I said. "He didn't have to obey you."

"Aidan ..."

"Like you said, pack before blood," I said, cutting him off. "He joined my team. He's part of my pack. If you really want to take him back for your ridiculous prosecution, my mate and I will consider sitting down and discussing it with you and Mom, but I'll tell you now, Jade has a soft spot for Tommy. She won't be handing him over to you." I wasn't entirely sure if that was true, but I knew Jade, and I knew, just knew that she wouldn't hand Tommy over whether she liked him or not.

"If you protect him, son, I'm done with you," Dad said, without a trace of emotion. "You sure you want that?"

"Yeah, Dad, I do," I said. "You were done with me years ago. What I do with Tommy won't change that." I sighed, shaking my head. "You take care of yourself, Dad." And with that, I hung up. It wasn't the first time he told me he was done with me, but right then, I decided it would be the last. And surprisingly enough, I was okay with that.

I fired off a quick text to Tommy: *Talked to my dad. Welcome to the Dog Mountain pack, buddy. We'll talk when you get back. Pack is meeting at my place. Moving out soon.*

And as I tucked my phone into my pocket, I found

myself wondering if he would make it back before we made our move on the cougars.

CHAPTER 13

JADE

The backyard was mostly deserted, with only Mark lurking nearby, watching me and the women who'd come with Erika. The air was crisp and clean, and leaves covered the grass in a layer of reds and oranges and greens, with only a few stragglers left clinging to the trees. Erika kicked at them, tossing the ones by her into a small pile, while I waited a little impatiently for her to get to whatever it was that she needed to tell me.

I was feeling a little on edge. After they'd barged into the house, they'd made a point about making sure Aidan wasn't home. Erika claimed that it was a woman's thing they needed me for and that they'd really prefer to talk to me without the male alpha and the team listening in, but my gut (and my inner-wolf) didn't believe her. Hence, the reason for Mark's lurking.

The other females hung around by her — all pack members. There was Whitney, a woman about my mother's age, with silky blond hair that hung past her shoulders and warm, inviting blue eyes. There was Kristen and Stacy, sisters, both in their late twenties, only a year apart. They kept their gazes respectfully dropped, waiting patiently, with their hands clasped behind their backs. There was also Laura, who I didn't know well. She was a newcomer to Dog Mountain, only been here for about nine months, and I thought it was probably the pack that had drawn her to our small town. And then there was Jo — short for ... well, I honestly didn't know what it was short for, but I thought it must be short for something — standing right beside Erika. She was the only one who constantly held my gaze. Her eyes were light green, and they were laughing, kind eyes that made me feel like she held all the secrets of the world and she was dying to tell me them.

I shuffled my weight to my right foot, as I surveyed them. I was a bit surprised that none of the women Erika brought were our age, and I didn't know what or if that meant anything. Erika typically clung to the pack members who were still in school, and it felt ... off that she was here without any of them.

"Erika, she's not going to wait forever," Jo said. Her voice was like bells, and it sounded as kind as her eyes looked. It was sweet and encouraging and full of mystery, and it washed away some of my unease by just hearing the sound. "It would be better if we had her support with this."

Erika said nothing.

"What's wrong?" I asked and stuck my hands in my pockets, not because they were cold, but because I felt an unbelievable need to fidget.

"We didn't say that anything was wrong," Jo murmured in that sweet, bell-like tone, but this time it didn't chase away the sense of foreboding that was starting to settle in my bones.

"You don't need to say it," I muttered. There were times, like this one in particular, that I hated being a werewolf. "I can smell your nerves. You all are on edge.

Is it me? Am I that unapproachable? I know the males had issues at first, but I thought you all were okay with me."

Erika groaned and cut me a dirty look. "Sorry if I seem a little nervous, but the last time I stood in front of you like this, you stripped me of my title." She didn't sound sorry, not even a little, and I really hadn't expected it, but suddenly, I felt bad for her.

"I needed you, Erika," I said and shook my head. "I don't know why, but I trusted you. God, I even liked you, and you lied to me." I wanted to say so much more, but I didn't. Now was definitely not the time, so instead, I asked, "Who's looking out for you today?"

"You mean who's babysitting me, right?" Her tone was sarcastic, and I gave her a look that clearly told her to cut it out. "Um, no one," she continued, more cautiously. "With everything going on, I guess you just forgot or whatever."

Crap! I felt my eyes widen. How could I forget something like that?

I opened my mouth, about to apologize, when Erika said, "It's okay. I'm good. The pack has mellowed out a lot since you and Aidan mated, and I made some friends."

"I can see that," I said, not sure of what else to say. The truth? I was feeling crazy guilty. Erika might not have been someone I actually liked, but she was still part of the pack, and it was me who'd put her in a compromising position by stripping her of her title. There was no excuse for my forgetting to assign someone to watch out for her, even if she was trying to brush it off as if it weren't a big deal.

"Erika came to us yesterday," Jo offered after a second of silence. "She had some ideas on this werecougar mess. Some really good ideas."

"Oh, yeah?" I didn't mean to sound dubious.

Honestly, I didn't. It just came out that way. I was sure that Erika could have good ideas. Really, I was. It was just, well, okay, maybe I was holding onto a little bit of a grudge.

Erika glanced vaguely in Mark's direction and then back to me. "Can you get rid of him for a few minutes?" Her voice was barely a whisper, and even with my sensitive ears, I almost missed what she said.

My first thought was to say no, but my gut, well, it was telling me that I needed to hear her out. "Mark," I called over my shoulder, "can you send someone to the store? Mom's going to freak if she doesn't get that stuff for breakfast."

Mark didn't look happy, but he did what I asked. With a jerk of his chin, he took off to the front of the house.

Once he was out of sight, I closed the ten-step distance between the females and me. When I stood in front of her, Erika offered a ghost of a smile and murmured, "Thank you."

I offered up a smile of my own that I hoped looked somewhat sincere and questioned gently, "So what's this idea?" Up close, I could see how tired she looked. Her eyes were ringed with gray shadows, and her complexion was paler than normal.

Erika hesitated for a second, took a deep breath, then blurted, "Well, yesterday when I was with Dom, he made this comment about how he didn't get why your dad hadn't brought more women in for his pack yet, and it got me thinking, maybe he hasn't told them that they won't be getting any of our wolves."

"Okay," I said. The sense of foreboding was coming back full force. "I'm not sure I like where you're going with this."

"Just hear her out, Jade," Jo said, smiling. She looked

sideways at Erika, raising her eyebrows. "Go on, doll. Tell her your idea."

Erika closed her eyes, swallowed hard, and then opened them again. She looked a little surer of herself, and firmly she said, "I thought that if they were still waiting for us, then maybe we should go to them."

"You want to go to them," I stated, not sure I understood. I looked around from one to the other and shook my head. They all seemed excited about this.

"I heard Beck talking last night," Erika said and made a face. "The children ... the little girl. How old do you think she needs to be before they ..." she broke off, swallowing hard and blinking fast. "I wasn't sure if I wanted to do this until then. Now I know I don't have a choice. I have to help. And I will any way I can."

"We'd make one hell of a distraction," Stacy interjected. "Just picture the six of us going in and shifting in front of all those men. I bet it would buy enough time for the team to get the kids out."

Okay, I had to admit that it was actually a pretty good idea. The women could go in. Strut around a little after shifting. It would definitely cause a distraction. But, Jesus, they could get hurt, or worse, they could actually end up in those cages if anything went wrong.

"The team, Aidan, they won't agree to this," I said carefully, not wanting them to think I was blowing them off. "You all know that, right?"

"They will if you're backing it," Laura countered, and I thought that she was entirely wrong on that.

"I think you all believe I hold more power over those boys than I actually do," I said, not unkindly, but with undeniable disbelief. "But," I huffed out a breath, "let's say you're right, and I can convince them, which just to be clear, I'm not saying I will, how do you plan on getting out of there once you're in?"

"The pack," they chorused excitedly.

I looked at them closely. God, they were serious. "Not much of a plan there."

"But it is," said Whitney. "We'll already be in there. When the team is done getting the kids out, the rest of the pack can move in with them. We can attack from both inside and out. It's perfect."

I settled my gaze on Erika. "Why are you doing this?"

"I screwed up," she said simply. "You gave me a second chance, and I want to prove that it wasn't wasted."

"Hey." Mark rounded the corner of the house and stalked over to us. He took one long look at me and asked, "You okay?"

"Yeah," I said, but I wasn't. I felt sick. A little light-headed and nauseated and really, really tense, which I totally blamed on worrying about what was going to happen as the day progressed. And it didn't help that I was starting to get a hunger headache. Maybe Mom was on to something with the frantic breakfast cooking.

Mark gave me one of those *I know you're lying* looks, but thankfully he didn't call me on it. "Aidan just called," he said. "He's on his way." He looked around our little group and smiled wickedly, if not conspiratorially, and right then, I had a sinking feeling that he'd overheard at least part of our conversation. He then confirmed it. "Just so you know, your idea is the best one I've heard yet." There was a mix of amusement and awe in his voice. "If you're sure about it, I'll back you."

"Mark," I snapped. I really wasn't sure that I wanted to encourage them in this plan. "They could get hurt."

"Yep, but they could get hurt when we attack

whether or not they act as a distraction," Mark said and turned back to the house.

No one noticed the sound of the footsteps clomping on the deck until it was too late.

CHAPTER 14

AIDAN

"This doesn't feel like a good idea," Dominic muttered again, looking out over the parking lot.

Looking back on it, I thought I probably should have known that Dominic wouldn't be fully on board with my plan. I'd admit it; there were a few problems with the whole thing. The main one, and the one that I thought Dominic was probably having the biggest problem with, was that I planned on bringing the entire pack with us. That would leave Dog Mountain and the humans within it completely unprotected while we were gone, which might not be the best idea since Jeff had sent cougars into town twice within the last twenty-four hours. But I was taking precautions against another attack — sort of.

The second one was returning the two cougars from the diner still breathing. I knew that was a risk. It would give us two more to fight against, but really, it was the only idea I had to gain access to their location without starting an immediate war. We needed to get the kids safe first, and my hope was that returning the dead with the living would make us look like we were trying to achieve some sort of peace.

"Dom, Jeff sounded really off," I said, looking over at him. "We need to act now." *Off* didn't really describe the desperation I'd heard in Jeff's voice, but I was trying a different approach, one that I seriously hoped Dominic would get, because flat out telling him that Jeff was desperate hadn't worked.

Dominic shook his head in disagreement and said nothing.

It had been about fifteen minutes since we'd made the calls for the pack to gather, and we were still waiting for a handful to arrive. Beck stood a good ten feet away from us, with Craig to his left. Pack members huddled around them, and Beck talked to them; a pep talk of sorts, except, it really wasn't all that peppy. It sounded more like a crash course on how to take someone down quickly. To him, efficiency seemed to be the key to killing, and the pack was eating it up, nodding and asking questions, seeking clarification on tactics. It was impressive and more than a little weird to see an enforcer dishing out the trade secrets, but damn, I was glad for it. Anything that could help prepare them, even if it might be a risk giving out those secrets, was worth it in my mind.

"What exactly is it that you don't like about it?" The question came out more annoyed than I'd meant, but what Dominic didn't seem to be getting was that I was also worried, really worried. Things could go wrong, and I wasn't naive enough to think that we could just charge in there, kill them all, and come out unscathed. Knowing that didn't leave me with a good feeling and having him doubt my plan made it even worse. In fact, I was feeling pretty low.

"I don't like any of it." He made a harsh buzzer kind of sound, and his eyes drifted back to the pack. "Tell me you've at least run this by Jade, and she's all in on it."

I drew in a deep breath and kicked at a random pebble. "Not yet," I said, and yeah, I sounded just as guilty as I felt. "But she'll be on board." Or at least I hoped she would be.

Dominic sighed and gave me a look. "Hope you're right," he said, and then he walked away.

I frowned and ran both hands through my hair, watching Dominic make his way over to Landon. He was off to the right, gathered under a large oak tree with two other pack members. They were huddled closely, listening intently as Landon prepped them on what they needed to accomplish.

As soon as the last few arrived, a scouting team, headed up by Landon, would take off, and the rest of us would head to my place to wait for their confirmation that all the cougars, or at least most of them, were at the hunting camp. I hated wasting time, but I couldn't take the entire pack away without ensuring they were all there. It would be risky and way too reckless with Jeff acting so unstable. I'd figured he'd make a move once Jade and I were mated; I just never thought it would be something like this, something so erratic and unplanned. He'd never struck me as the desperate type. Clearly, I'd read him wrong. But then, with Jade's freak-out yesterday, I guessed that was enough to push him over the edge. It was surely enough to make him aware that we'd never been playing into his game.

I took my phone out of my pocket and woke the screen. 10:05. It felt like it should have been a hell of a lot later. Only two hours ago, we'd been sitting at the diner about to have breakfast and trying to figure out what to do with the team. Those two hours felt like a lifetime ago.

This is going to work, I thought. *It has to work.*

Fall in Dog Mountain really was beautiful. Even

with most of the leaves fallen from the trees and scattered on the ground, the area was full of browns, greens, oranges, and reds. *Nature at its finest moment*, I thought. The air was chilly, but warmer than first thing this morning. There was a good fall breeze pushing through the parking lot, and the sun was out full force, bringing out a shine in the thawing asphalt.

I looked back at my phone and scrolled through my contacts, looking for Mark's number. I thumbed the screen and brought it to my ear when I found it. He answered on the second ring and said, "Tell me you're on your way here."

I laughed once. "That doesn't sound encouraging, Mark," I said. "I was really hoping that it would be safe to show my face there by now."

Mark made an exasperated sound. "Depends on what you mean by safe. Jade told Pam everything, and Pam deals with stress by cooking."

"That doesn't sound so bad." And it didn't, mainly because I was starving. Food would definitely be a good thing right now, and Pam's cooking was amazing. Actually, hearing she was working out her issues by cooking was probably the best news I'd gotten all day.

"Dude, you're going to need to buy another freezer for all the leftovers, and you won't have to cook for months."

That made me laugh. Hard. "It can't be that bad."

"I'm not joking," Mark said. "I just had to send the two guys that came with us to the store for more food. She's cooked everything you had. And that's not all. Erika showed up with five other females demanding to talk to Jade. She's outback with them now."

"Erika's at my house with Jade." It wasn't really a question, more of a stunned statement.

"Yep and those women are all hyped up about something."

That scared me a little bit. Erika and hyped-up wasn't a good combination. Add Jade, Marcy, and Pam, all totally stressed out, and then add another five women to the mix. Well, that sounded like a disaster just waiting to happen. And it was with that thought that I remembered that I never did ask Dominic about the way he'd been watching Erika at the funeral home yesterday.

"Who's supposed to be watching her today?" I asked him, surprised that my voice sounded calm because I sure as hell wasn't feeling it.

"Not sure," Mark said. "Beck dropped her off at the headquarters this morning before going to meet you."

My jaw clenched, and I felt a bud of anger bloom within me. "Let Jade know I'm leaving in a few, and Mark, the rest of the pack's coming with me."

"It's happening now, then," Mark said, in a frighteningly steady tone, not at all unnerved with the possibility of killing or being killed. But then, that was the enforcer mentality, protect the pack at all costs.

"Yep, I've got to go," I said hastily and hung up because Landon was walking toward me, and he didn't look happy.

I studied Landon for a beat, trying and failing to get a read on exactly how unhappy he was, then I pushed off the wall and went to meet him. When we were a few feet apart, I jerked my chin and asked, "What's up?"

In the next second, though, it became clear that he wasn't unhappy — he was focused. "We've got to get moving," he said, with false patience. "Where are the other pack members?"

"Seems Beck didn't bother to make sure someone was here to take over the Erika watch before dropping her off this morning," I said very quietly. *Shit*, I was already restless, so was my inner-wolf, and whatever crap Erika was pulling with running to my mate made it so, so much worse. I felt a growl building inside me, the beast clawing at my chest. Jade had enough on her plate dealing with her mom; she didn't need Erika adding to it. "Erika brought them to see Jade."

Landon considered my words and nodded as if my house seemed like a perfectly reasonable place for them to be, and if Erika hadn't been with them, it probably would have been. "What about Tommy?"

"Nothing yet," I said and sighed. "Can't keep waiting for him."

"No, we can't," Landon agreed, but he sounded less than enthusiastic about it. "Would have been good to have him, though. Another trained enforcer ..." He shrugged. "He would have come in handy."

He was right. He would have. I didn't doubt that for a moment, but we couldn't keep waiting. Jeff had already sent two groups of cougars into Dog Mountain since yesterday, and I doubted he'd stop until we'd killed his entire pack, or they killed us.

I was aware of Dominic coming up behind me, and by the anger, I caught in his scent, I figured he was most likely glaring and shaking his head. Landon's eyes slid past me to focus on him, and his fierce, focused expression faltered.

"You ready for this?" I asked him, drawing his attention away from Dominic.

Landon's grin was tight and predatory when he looked back at me. "Always," he said, and I had no doubt he meant it.

CHAPTER 15

Mark was halfway across the backyard when the creaky front door opened. He seemed to hesitate in his step for a second as if the sound caught him off guard, and it struck me as odd. We were expecting Aidan, and Mark had just sent someone to the store. People on the deck and the door opening didn't seem odd to me, but his reaction to the sound had my inner-wolf doing backflips in my belly and the hair along my neck prickling my skin.

And that was when I realized that I hadn't heard a vehicle, and it was at that moment that Mark started to run.

Things fell together.

It had only been minutes, five at the most, since whoever was sent to the store left, nowhere near enough time to get there and back. And Aidan, he was coming from the pack headquarters, and he'd only just left. Even speeding, it would take ten minutes to get home.

It took me less than a second to put it together, but by then, Mom was already screaming, and so was Marcy, and I couldn't breathe. A chill took hold of

me. All my training, all my skills were suddenly just ...
gone. Terror wound around me, washing over me and
my legs; they just wouldn't work.

Until ... they did.

And I was moving, running for the back door, and
my breath was pushing in and out of my lungs in harsh
pants.

"No!" Erika got in my way fast. "No, you can't just
run in there." She grabbed me, her hand squeezing
tightly around my forearm, and she began yanking me
backward, further away from Mom and Marcy and the
house.

"I have to," I shrieked, digging my feet into the
ground and pulling against her hold. Panic gripped me.
Mark was already gone. Vanished inside the house, but
the screaming was still screeching through my ears.

Wolves surrounded Erika and me. Closing in,
circling. There were five of them, and it took me a
second to realize through my panic-induced haze that
they were the women I'd just been speaking to.

My wolves.

They were growling. Lips curled, razor-sharp teeth
bared. Their heads were turned, watching the house as
they positioned themselves around me. *Protecting me*, I
thought, but as I listened to the screaming, protection
was the last thing I wanted. Marcy and Mom, they were
the ones who needed protecting, not me.

"Go help, Mark!" There was no mistaking the
command in my tone. The wolves didn't hesitate, not
even a little. All five of them lunged forward as a unit,
tearing across the grass toward the house.

I started to follow, but Erika's hands clenched
tighter on my forearm. Tight enough to bruise. "Jade,
don't," she pleaded, sounding desperate and scared.

I looked at her hand, the angle she was gripping me
from. I took a breath, tried to calm myself enough to

think, and as I let it out, I saw it clearly. All I had to do was twist to the right and yank, and I'd be free of her. And that's exactly what I did.

Erika made a gasping pain-filled sound and pulled her hand back, and before she could shake off the tweak I'd caused in her wrist, I was running again.

An overwhelming smell of blood was the first thing I noticed as I ran into the house, and then I noticed the screaming had changed to whimpering. I could hear growling coming from upstairs and slapping and struggling from the kitchen.

The smell of cougar, sour, lemon, cat, with a hint of birch bark, hit me next. My nostrils flared, and I let out a growl as my gaze landed on a man moving through the living room toward me. He was tall and built like a flippin' tank, moving fast.

I didn't have time to shift before he was on me, although with the way my skin was shuddering, I thought my inner-wolf didn't agree. Adrenaline pounded through my veins, fast and hot, and I braced myself for impact.

But he didn't crash into me. The man stopped just before hitting me, and his hands shot out, curling around my neck, squeezing, and cutting off my air pipe. "I've got her," he shouted.

I didn't think, just reacted. I let the adrenaline take hold of me and focused it all on my hands, picturing claws sprouting from my fingertips. I felt the rush as my nails lengthened and thickened, and as my partial shift finished, I took a swipe at his eyes.

He let out a feral scream and dropped his hands from my throat. I doubled over, gasping for air.

"You little bitch." The growled voice hit my ears a second before I was knocked down, and then the man was on top of me, straddling my stomach.

I bucked up and swiped out again with my claws,

dragging them down his neck. He struggled to grab hold of my wrists, but I kept bucking and moving, and he kept missing his target, coming up with only air between his fingers as I continued to attack his throat.

Blood dripped down onto me. Onto my face. Staining my clothes. I could hear the wolves in the house. Scrambling claws on the floors. Growls. Snarls. Busy fighting their own battles. Mom was screaming again from what sounded like the kitchen, and I bucked harder. I needed to get to her. I needed to help her.

The man took hold of my left wrist, slamming it down to the floor and pinning it above my head. He grinned and opened his mouth to speak, but he didn't get a chance to. I swiped out again with my other hand and dug my claws deep into his throat.

His eyes widened as I tore my hand free, and his hands shot up clutching at the wound. He made a gurgling sound. My stomach heaved as more blood fell onto me, and I shoved him off. He fell to the floor, choking on the blood that must have been pooling in his throat from the gashes and tears I'd given him.

I scrambled back and shot to my feet, expecting him to come at me again, but he didn't. His throat ... God, I'd torn his throat wide open, and he'd stopped choking and gurgling. And he wasn't moving.

He's dead, I thought numbly. *I killed him.*

Mark appeared beside me, causing me to jump. I had no clue where he'd come from, my house seriously wasn't big enough to sneak up on someone, but somehow he had. He looked at the man and nodded what I thought was approval, and then he held a finger to his lips, telling me to keep quiet, and pointed to the stairs.

A man, medium build, sort of bland, with pasty skin, pale hair, and washed blue jeans, chose that moment to pull my mom from the kitchen. He spotted us, dropped his hold on Mom, and he moved faster than anyone I had ever seen. It was so quick that I didn't even see what had happened. One moment Mark was standing beside me, and the next, he was on the ground. The man went with him, holding him down with his knee pressed into Mark's throat.

I screamed. I couldn't help it, but it turned out that my scream was the right thing to do. Two wolves, one gray and the other light brown came barreling down the stairs, and I suddenly wished I had screamed when the tank had been on top of me.

I didn't even have time to think of shifting before they were on the man, tearing him from Mark, and as soon as he was free, Mark was on his feet. And the man was screaming and kicking at the wolves that were ripping through the flesh and muscles in his calves and thighs.

There was blood. So much blood, staining the carpet and flinging onto the walls. But the man, he was covered in blood, too. His face, his shirt, and it wasn't all fresh, I realized. It wasn't all his.

Mark stood in front of him for a moment, watching the carnage. His face was blank, absolutely void of expression, but then his eyes flared. In a quick motion, Mark reached out, grabbed the man's head, and twisted, and he stopped screaming.

The wolves let go as the man flopped lifelessly to the floor, and they leaped back upstairs. That was when I noticed that I hadn't moved. Not even an inch. I was shaking, and Mom ... I could hear Mom crying.

"Where's Mac?" I asked Mark. My voice sounded calm. Too calm. *I should be freaking out,* I thought, staring down at a man I'd never met, another dead man in my house. But I wasn't freaking out. I felt numb. Completely and totally numb.

"The other one has her upstairs." Mark's voice was growled, and he was already pounding up the stairs.

I spun, about to follow him, when I heard the front door creak, and my gaze snapped to the man who was filling the doorway. My father.

He scanned the room with a quick, thorough glance, and his face twisted up with rage. "Jesus, Jade. You killed them?" His voice was scary calm, not matching his expression. "What's wrong with you?"

I almost told him that I'd only killed the one, but I caught myself and shrugged instead. "They attacked me, Dad. They attacked Mom, too. I was defending myself, my house, and my mother."

His eyes went to Mom, and they darkened with fury. My eyes slid to her, too. She was a sobbing puddle on the floor, halfway between him and me. I didn't think. I ran to her, placing myself directly in between them, and I snapped my gaze back to him.

We stared at each other in tense, angry silence for a few seconds before Dad spoke. "I'd never hurt you or your mother, Jade," he snapped.

"No, you'd just let your monsters do it for you." My inner-wolf was snarling, begging to be let out, but somehow, and I really didn't know how I held her back.

"Jade, I'd never ..." He sighed. "Aidan, he's not thinking clearly. We came here to reason with him. I swear. No one was meant to get hurt."

I said nothing because clearly, that was a lie. Mom and Marcy wouldn't have been screaming if that were true, and there wouldn't be two dead men on my living room floor.

He must have taken my silence as some kind of an invitation because he raised his hands as he stepped into the house, inching the front door shut behind him. "All I've ever wanted was to join our packs, Jade. Wolves and cougars, and more. We could all live together, work together. We could be unstoppable. And Dog Mountain, with the pack living out in the open like they do, it's the perfect place to start. I'm not the monster you think I am."

I laughed, a shocking sound that just blurted out even though I tried really hard to swallow it. "Don't lie to me. The wolves only exposed themselves because of your pack. To keep this town safe from your cougars."

He shrugged. "Times change. We don't care about getting our territory back. That's not what's important now. Uniting shifters is."

"Dog Mountain has never been yours," I spat, not even bothering to acknowledge the rest. There was nothing he could say that would make me consider letting my pack join him and his cougars. I was so sure that it wasn't worth the breath to refute it.

"It was." He dropped his gaze from mine, and I swore he almost looked sad. And if he hadn't glanced back up at me right then, I would have believed he was, but his eyes gave him away. They were cold and flat and unfeeling. "Over one-hundred years ago now, but it was. We were pushed out when the werewolves settled here."

"I don't believe you." It would have been a scream, except that I couldn't get the breath to make that happen. My lungs were just as numb as the rest of me, and I found it hard to pull in any air.

Dad's face flushed an angry red. "Look at what Aidan's doing to us! Look at what he's turned you into. A killer. Tiffany. Jared. They're both dead because of you. And you've just taken two more lives. This is Aidan's fault. All of it. He's turned you against me."

"Get out," Mom said in a small, broken voice. "Just get out." She was still crying, soft, small sobs, and she was still tucked behind me, sitting on the floor right where the man had dropped her.

If Dad heard her, he didn't let on. "Jade, I love you. Please help me. I can't lose my daughter. Please." He stretched out a hand to me, and damn, but I wanted to take it. For half a second, I hesitated. He sounded so sincere, so desperate, that I really wanted to believe him. And I thought he knew that because he smiled a little and took a hesitant step toward me as he continued with his plea. "You're an alpha of this pack. You have his scent now. You can help stop all of this."

I was vaguely aware of the others filing into the living room, and I thought they must have killed the other man that was upstairs because it was really, really quiet in the house suddenly. Only breathing and heartbeats and soft, breathless crying were left.

I swallowed hard. Dad had that look on his face. The one that was always there when I was upset. It was the one that made me want to rush to him and jump into one of his bear hugs. But when I looked into his eyes, really looked, they were still flat, unfeeling, and my heart broke all over again.

"The women ..." My throat clogged up as tears bit at my eyes. I watched him, waiting, desperately wanting him to explain that. It was horrible, but I thought I would have taken anything at that point. Anything to make my heart stitch back together. If it meant that I could keep my dad, mate, and pack. For that sick, twisted second, I thought I would have taken any explanation no matter what it was.

But he didn't have the courtesy to look even a little sorry as he said, "I've been trying to change that."

As it turned out, I wouldn't take just any explanation.

"I've heard," I said. Bile rose up my throat. "Wolves heal faster, right? Less of a chance of us dying on you."

Dad's face went red again, and when he spoke, it

looked as if it were a struggle for him not to shout. "Jade, where did you ..."

He didn't get a chance to finish. A savage cry split through the room, and Erika launched herself at him. She shoved him back a step and then cocked her arm back and punched him. Her fist connected with a meaty slap, and he fell back, landing with a thud.

"Don't you dare try to deny it, you bastard!" Erika shrieked. "I was there. I recorded your meeting with Tiffany. We've all seen it! We have proof!"

Erika closed the few steps to where my dad had landed and stood over him. She was vibrating, her hands clenched tight, and her stance, well, she looked as if she were about to kick him.

"Erika!" I shouted. Adrenaline rushed through me — hot and raw. My scent gathered in the air, my imprint heated, and my inner-wolf began to fight me for control. My skin started to shudder, and I knew, just knew, if I didn't pull it together, I'd end up a wolf, and that would not help this situation. I swallowed hard and forced every bit of command I had into my tone as I said, "Enough!"

I wasn't entirely sure if it was Erika I was trying to command or if it was my inner-wolf, but both listened. Erika slid back a step but never took her eyes off my dad, and my inner-wolf backed down, letting me take the lead.

"Why are you doing this, Dad?" My voice came out whisper soft, and I cleared my throat loudly. "The attacks ... the women ... why? I need you to tell me why!"

He held my gaze, and his face contorted with frustration. "I already told you, Jade. I want the shifter community to come together."

"That explains nothing!" I sucked in a breath, trying to rein in my building fury. "Those women weren't shifters. They had nothing to do with your little plan."

"Those women kept my pack happy," he spat, glaring up at me with something that looked a heck of a lot like hatred.

My eyes blurred and prickled. It was at that moment that I realized my father was beyond saving. He was gone. Completely and totally lost within his delusional thoughts. "I don't even know who you are anymore."

"Jade ..." Dad started, but I didn't let him finish because I honestly didn't think I could take any more of his lies.

"You've still got time to run, Dad," I said. "Aidan's on his way home. You better do it while you can. He'll know you were here, and he'll come after you. So run and don't stop because he'll keep hunting you. And you know what? I'm not going to stop him anymore."

"Jade," Erika started to protest, and I held up a hand, stopping her.

I glared at my father and said, "You have three seconds before I let her kill you."

Dad's mouth opened and then closed. He wiped some blood from the corner of his lips and said, "You're making a big mistake, Jade." And then he shocked the hell out of me.

He shifted.

And it wasn't into a big cat.

He shrunk in size, foot by foot. Bones broke, and wings, big feathery wings, sprung from his back.

I blinked, and when my eyes opened again, a hawk hovered in front of me. He beat his wings a few times slowly, holding in place, and then he flew out the back door, which was still wide open.

CHAPTER 16

It took another three minutes for Aidan to show up after my father flew — *oh my God, he flew* — away.

Mark and I had ushered everyone outside, away from the death and the blood, and that was where we were waiting when Aidan drove up. He wasn't alone. Car after car pulled up into the driveway and onto the grass, and soon our whole front yard was filled with pack members.

Three minutes too late to help.

Aidan got out of a car, so did Beck. He was looking at Beck, laughing at something he'd said. He glanced at the house. His eyes caught mine. He smiled, waved, and then his smile turned scary, somehow. It was all sharp edges and contorted curves. Forced. Wrong. His gaze darted to Mom, sitting on the steps with Marcy huddled in her arms. Then to Mark standing behind them with a hand on Mom's shoulder. Then to Erika and the other women, standing on the grass off to the left of the porch.

His nostrils flared; I thought he was probably catching the scent of the enemy, or maybe he could smell how freaked out we all were. His brown eyes came back to me, and his face went blank, completely and utterly blank, except for his eyes. His eyes were filled with emotion, so much emotion that they were almost scarier than his smile.

"Jade, are you okay?" His voice was hesitant as if he really wasn't sure how to assess the situation. I was sure it looked a bit strange, all of us hanging out in front of the house. I was sure he could see the blood splattered on most of us, and Marcy and Mom were sobbing quietly.

No, I'm not okay. I just saw my dad change into a bird, and there are dead werecougars in my house. That's what I wanted to say, but what I did was shrug, and my voice was all wrong, small and sad and weak, when I said, "I think so."

Aidan took a step, and then he was running, colliding into me, locking me in a breathtakingly tight embrace, so tight that I couldn't even get my arms loose and hug him back. "Tell me you're okay," he said. His voice was tight and growled, and his grip got impossibly tighter.

People were moving around us. Opening the door, going into the house. Growls. Voices. Some shouted. Some whispered. It was suddenly loud, really loud, and it wasn't until Aidan loosened his grip and I snapped my gaze up that I realized I hadn't told him what he wanted to hear.

"I'm okay," I said, and damn, but there were tears in my voice. I swallowed hard and blinked fast, and my voice (thankfully) was stronger when I tried again. "We're all fine, but um ..." I bit my lip and looked to the front door. I opened my mouth, about to tell him what had happened, and probably more importantly, I was going to tell him that I'd let my father get away, but what came out was completely different. "I think we need a new bed, and we definitely need to rip out the nasty carpet in the living room. They're both covered in blood, and, um, there are kind of three dead cougars in human form in the house."

He cupped my face in his big, warm palms and brought my eyes back to his. "Don't care about the bed or the carpet, sweetheart," he said, a small smirk playing at the corner of his lips. He shook his head as if he couldn't believe I was worried about those things. "I don't care if the whole house needs to be torn down and rebuilt. You are the only thing that matters to me." And then he kissed me, and it was full of passion and fear and need, and I was clutching onto him, and him onto me, and for those few seconds, I completely forgot that the pack was all standing by.

But then it ended, and he decided to let me breathe again, although it was a ragged breath at best. He brushed his thumbs across my cheeks, and his expression changed to serious. "Tell me what happened," he said, and with those four words, reality came crashing back.

I told him everything.

Mom put her overcooking to use. With Dominic's help (she refused to go back into the house, not that I blamed her), they fed the pack the food she'd already cooked. They'd found a long, plastic folding table in the garage, along with what I thought had to be a year's supply of throwaway plates and cups and set it up in the backyard. It was loaded with a mix of fruit, eggs, bacon, and pancakes. There were also a lot of steamed vegetables, batches of cookies, and muffins, and I even spotted the ground beef that had been in the freezer and all the fixings for tacos laid out.

While they were setting up the feast, Aidan explained why he'd brought the pack along with the two cougars from the diner, who were currently tied and gagged in the garage, home. He had a plan — a plan that was already in motion. And although the plan was no better or worse than Erika's idea, I really didn't know how to feel about him sending Landon out with only two other wolves without even telling me first.

I tried a few times to tell him about Erika's idea, except I didn't think he listened. He was excited and kind of hyper, and he kept telling me how *huge* it was that my dad was a full shifter (not that I had any clue what that meant), but it seemed to explain a lot to him. I also had to admit that even though he was excited and it was kind of hard to keep his attention, I hadn't tried overly hard to make him listen to me either. Replacing one semi-okay plan with another semi-okay plan didn't make a whole lot of sense, and Aidan was pretty busy trying to organize everyone, so yeah, I didn't really try too hard to get it out.

When Aidan went to help pull the dead from the house and load them in the truck, I snuck away. I needed a moment, or maybe ten, to pull myself together. I felt pretty shaky and really confused, and I was just plain tired. Tired of fighting. Tired of being scared. I was also tired of caring about what happened to my dad.

Numbness would be better, I thought. And right then, I was also feeling pretty numb.

I was standing on the back porch watching my wolves practice their fighting techniques when I felt his hands grip my hips and his chest press against my back. It was a familiar scene in front of me. One I'd participated in countless times, except it had been Jared barking out the instructions, not Beck and Craig, and I'd been the wolf getting my butt kicked.

Aidan's breath was warm against the back of my neck, sending small shivers along my skin. His hands rested lightly on my hips, holding me close against him. He didn't say anything for a long moment, and when he did, it was a whisper in my ear. "How are you holding up?" he asked. He seemed a little calmer, but I was pretty sure he was just trying to mask the excitement he was feeling for my benefit.

"I think I'm pretty much numb," I said, and then, not wanting to explore that topic any further, I continued with, "Thankfully, Mom won't go back into the house, so the cooking has stopped. And the pack's eating everything she already made, so it looks like we won't have to go shopping for a freezer."

Aidan chuckled, a deep, throaty sound that made my knees soft. "I have some good news for you," he murmured as his lips grazed the side of my neck with gentle presses that made my stomach flutter a little.

"Oh, yeah," I said. "What's that?"

He leaned back against the house, pulling me with him. "The team and I are good."

I tilted my head back to look at him and rolled my eyes. "Yeah, I noticed that." And I had, pretty much the moment he'd gotten out of the car and I saw him laughing at something Beck had said. I didn't think I'd ever seen Aidan laugh with one of the enforcers, and I knew I'd never seen one of them try to make him laugh. But them getting along (even if it was awesome) was not really important. Not after finding out my father was not what I thought he was.

Silence fell, and I leaned back, resting my head against his shoulder. I felt sick to my stomach and tired, really, really tired. I tried hard to stay relaxed against him, but cold panic kept jerking at my muscles. I knew, just knew, that he had to hate me for letting my dad go. How couldn't he? If I were him, I'd probably hate me, too. And once his hyperness wore off, he would. I was sure of it.

My hands were shaking, so I folded my arms across

my chest in an attempt to hide it. I pulled in a breath, let it out, and broke the silence. "Tell me I didn't screw up."

Aidan actually laughed. "You're kidding me, right? Of course, you didn't screw up."

"Now say it like you mean it," I shot back, shocked, and well, it hurt, like a lot, that he was laughing at me. I tried to wiggle out of his arms, but he held on, his hands moving from my hips to coil around my waist with relentless strength.

"You found out that he can shift into more than just a cougar," he said, an animated pitch coming out in his voice. "That's something, Jade. It's huge, actually. A piece we didn't have before. It explains so much. Like why I couldn't pick up his scent. He's not just one animal. He could be any of them. All of them. It confuses the smells, hides them, and changes them. I should have figured it out. We had a full-blown shifter in my dad's pack when I was seven. If anyone screwed up, it was me. Again."

I wasn't entirely sure what he was talking about, but I knew he was trying to be reasonable, trying to make me feel better. And it was a super nice gesture. It just sucked, though, that it didn't help my trembling hands. "For the record, I'm not sure what you're talking about with the more than one animal smell thing, and I only found out that he could do that because I let him walk away."

Aidan didn't try to explain the animal/smell thing. Instead, he gave me a little squeeze and said, "He's your dad, sweetheart, and your mom was here. I imagine that if it were my dad and my mom was there, I'd do the same thing."

"No, you wouldn't," I said. I swallowed a bubble of panic and tried really hard to make my voice sound reasonable, just like his, and when I spoke again, I even thought I succeeded, sort of. "You hate your father."

"But I love my mother." Again with a reasonable tone. "On the plus side," he continued with a smile in his voice, "we now have a good reason not to put off ripping out that nasty ass carpet."

"Yeah, I guess." I was starting to feel drowsy and almost content leaning against him, but it was hard to completely relax with the sounds of the wolves training in the yard. A constant reminder of what was still to come.

Aidan chuckled and kissed the side of my neck, just below my ear. "What was Erika doing here?" He kept it at a bare whisper as if he wasn't sure he'd really meant to voice the question out loud.

"I tried to tell you earlier," I said. "She had an idea."

"Erika." He sounded surprised, and I tilted my head to the side to see his forehead scrunched up. His eyebrows rose as he looked down at me. "Erika had an idea?"

"Yeah." I dropped my head again and rested it on his shoulder, and then with a long sigh, I told him the idea.

Aidan said nothing when I finished, and I wasn't entirely sure what to make of the change in his scent. It was still heavy with that hyper excitement, but there was something else there now, something I just couldn't place, spicing it up.

His arms dropped from my waist, and I slowly turned around. His face was set, deep in thought, and when he met my eyes, he gave his head a little shake and laughed, a startling kind of sound, and said, "I like it."

"You. Like. It," I repeated slowly, narrowing my eyes. "How can you like this idea?" *But I already knew the answer,* I thought *because it really was a great plan.*

"It could work, Jade." He was staring down at me, but I didn't really think he saw me. His eyes sort of hazed over, and his expression intensified to what I thought of as his *thinking face.* He leaned forward and kissed my cheek absently, and then he walked away. He made it about ten steps before turning back and sending me a quick, unreadable glance. "Come on, Jade. Landon's going to be back anytime now. We need to get ready."

I wasn't sure what *get ready* meant, but I followed him on aching legs down the steps and into the yard, figuring I was probably about to find out.

CHAPTER 17

AIDAN

The yard was as busy as a mall before Christmas. Pack members were gathering in clusters, some looked excited and some right out worried, but all of them were here, and they were all ready to move the second Landon got back.

There was a good-sized group of them in wolf form, training with Beck and Craig. They were like drill sergeants, breaking out training exercises over and over. It was amazing seeing the pack work like this. Together. As a unit. When they did, they looked as if they could take down anything in their path. And I was counting on just that.

"Dom," I called and waved a hand for him to come over when I spotted him in wolf form, running through a drill with Luken. They both stopped at the sound of my voice, and Dominic glanced my way, just a quick turn of his head before he deliberately turned his back to me and squared off with Luken again.

I heard Jade stumble down the steps, following me. I glanced over my shoulder as she did a little hop-skip, catching her balance. She shot me a flustered and slightly confused smile and jogged to catch up.

"What's up with him?" she asked warily as she reached me.

I cut her a quick sideways look and grinned. "He's giving me the silent treatment, I think. He's not a fan of my plan." I was too wired to really care. Completely wound up. My entire body was buzzing with energy. My hands, my legs, even the inside of my stomach felt like a live wire, sparking and tingling.

"I'm not entirely sure I like it either." She laughed. It was just a little laugh, and it sounded panicked. "I'm also not even sure I know what it is anymore."

I stayed silent, searching the clusters for Erika. My head was just too full to try and get anything out. Jade's dad was a shifter. A full-blown shifter. That was big. Huge. And Erika's plan, combined with mine ... I had to tell her. Had to talk to her. I needed every little detail.

Jade waited for a moment, and then she let out a long, dramatic sigh. "You want me to talk to him?"

"Nope. He'll get over it." I finally spotted Erika tucked away under a tree while I continued scanning the yard. "Come on, we need to chat with Erika." I reached out and took her hand, and together we skirted the yard.

When I'd first met Jeff, I thought something was wrong with me. I felt like I was losing my senses. I'd been going crazy these last few weeks trying to figure out why I couldn't smell his animal. Had he been taking some kind of drug that masked his scent? Or was there some kind of herb he was using? I knew it had to be something, and I knew it wasn't just me. My pack didn't smell the cougar in him either. But the reason had been simple. The reason was his species.

Jade didn't get it. I knew I probably should have taken the time to try and explain it to her better. But really, I didn't know much more than what I'd already said. Shifters, real, full shifters, carried only the scent of the form they were in while they were in it. It had something to do with the multiple animal thing. That's what the shifter from my dad's pack had told me when I was a kid, and even to him, it had been a mystery of sorts. He'd called it nature, but I remember telling him it was magic.

Damn, I couldn't believe I hadn't put it together. It was all there, staring me right in the face. But in my defense, I hadn't come across a full shifter since I was seven, and that was a long time ago.

What Jeff had said about the wolf pack pushing them out of Dog Mountain could very well be true. From what I'd been told about the Dog Mountain pack history, the cougars had been around tormenting them from before Jeff was even born. And Richard had said the same thing before he died. It would explain the bad blood between my pack and his.

I wondered if the cougars even knew what he was. Shifters weren't a common species to come across. But as Jeff told Jade, times change, so maybe they did know. Maybe he'd promised them world domination or some crap like that, and with the rest of the stuff, he'd spewed at Jade about uniting shifters and being unstoppable ... Well, it kind of made sense that they did know. So even though she told him to run, my gut told me he didn't go far.

And that was exactly why Erika's plan was brilliant. With a few tweaks, we could make it look like Jade had a change of heart after seeing her father. She could deliver the females as a peace offering. The first step in uniting our packs. It was perfect.

But really, uniting shifters was a joke. There was a reason why packs didn't mix, especially wolves. We were too damn territorial. Another pack coming in, all it would lead to is one big pissing contest. Sure, we could work together when necessary, but even then, it wasn't an entirely comfortable union, and it typically ended as soon as the job was done.

The whole unstoppable thing was a joke, too. What did he think? We'd just come out in the open and take over the world? Even if he managed to get enough shifters on board, humans would be an entirely different story. Dog Mountain was unique. They accepted us probably because we didn't let our pack business spill too much into their day-to-day lives. But humans as a whole, in big numbers, they'd panic. And they had a whole lot of guns and testing facilities. Shifters, Weres, we'd never stand a chance against human technology when that panic set in.

So what would that leave him? Maybe he'd be able to rule the shifters. Maybe a few were-packs would join in. But in the end, he'd still be nothing. A blip on the map.

Erika was sitting, tucked under a tree, watching Craig's every movement as if it were the last time she'd ever see him, and she was trying to commit it all to memory. As we reached her, Jade squeezed my hand tightly. I didn't know if it was some kind of warning or her nerves, but I rubbed my thumb in small circles on her palm between our clasped hands, figuring it might soothe her either way and said, "Hey, Erika."

Erika startled and looked up at me with wide eyes. "Oh, hey," she said and faked a smile as she glanced between Jade and me before she let her gaze fall back to Craig.

I watched her faze us out as if she'd already forgotten we were there, and I wondered if she knew how damaged she looked. *Probably not.* It was like her heart wasn't just broken but had been torn clean out and was lying at her feet.

Seeing her damaged managed to tamp down my

excitement and made me feel like a piece of crap because it was partly my fault that Craig wouldn't speak to her. I let go of Jade's hand, crouched down beside her, and placed a hand on her bent knee. "If you want to talk to him, I'll pull him out of there. Mark could take over."

Erika considered it and then shrugged. "Nah, it'd just piss him off." She noticed Jade looking at my hand and quickly brushed it from her knee. The fake smile made another appearance. "Besides, it's just hit 11:00. Landon will be here any time now. No point in Craig wasting his anger on me when he could use it fighting."

I glanced up at Jade. I was completely lost on what to do here. I didn't know if this was some secret girl code like the word *fine*, which I knew from experience meant anything but *fine*, or if Erika was serious and she really didn't want to talk to Craig.

Jade watched us for a long second before she slowly bent down and sat beside Erika. She kept her expression carefully still as Erika shimmied back from me. She didn't want to scare her, I realized.

When Erika stopped squirming, she said, "I told Aidan about your idea." Her tone was soothing, sweet even, and just as fake as Erika's smile. "He said he likes it."

Erika glanced at me and hesitated. "You like it?" She blinked and smiled for real. "Really?"

I grinned, and the excitement started to bubble up again. I was about to tell her and Jade the new plan that was forming in my mind when Craig, his voice growled, asked from behind me, "What's going on here?"

Right, I thought. He was always watching her, too, even if she didn't realize it. My grin widened at the stunned look on Erika's face as her eyes slid past me to look at him.

I glanced over my shoulder and said, "Grab Beck and Mark and tell Dominic to get over his issues and get over here. There's been a change in plans."

JADE

It was nearly 11:15 when Dominic finally shifted and joined us. Fifteen long minutes and my heart was still beating wildly in my throat. I wasn't sure I liked hyper Aidan. Actually, it was kind of unnerving.

Dominic paused at the edge of our little meeting, and when he noticed that Aidan hadn't waited for him, I thought he looked disappointed for a quick second, but then his closed-off mask fell back in place.

The pack had formed a semi-circle around Aidan, listening as he explained what we would do. Heads nodded. Grunted agreements sounded. They liked it. Really liked it. And it made me feel sick with worried nerves.

I can do this, I thought, swallowing hard. It was a piece of cake, and I wouldn't be alone. The pack would be close by. The women would be with me. *I can do this.*

I was standing off to the side of the gathering with Marcy and Mom. Marcy clung to my hand. She was shaking, her hand trembling within mine. "He's kind of scary focused," she said in a hushed whisper.

"I know," I whispered back because he was. I thought it was more than just focused, though. He commanded attention. He was determined. He was ready for war. And his vibe summoned the same reaction from the pack. Everyone seemed just as ramped up as he was.

"Jade," Beck said, causing me to blink and look up. He gave me a look as if he were expecting me to answer a question.

"Yes?" I said, and I was sure my face was utterly blank. I felt my heart flutter madly with panic that I'd missed something important. "Sorry, what?"

He grinned that *you're a pain in the ass* grin he had just for me. "Are you good driving Jared's old truck?"

The truck was a monster. It was huge. I hated riding in the passenger seat, and I really wasn't looking forward to attempting to maneuver it down a narrow, hardly used dirt road. I swallowed. "I think so. But I want one of you guys with me so my driving it won't be an issue."

"I don't know about that," Mark said. "I think it might look suspicious."

I quickly shook my head. "No, it wouldn't. I'm just there to deliver the goods. And besides," I shrugged, "I'm also the alpha female. It would look suspicious if I went alone. They'd expect me to bring someone, wouldn't they?"

"His new idea is to send you." Dominic's voice was deathly calm, and his eyes sparked. He tilted his head to look at me. "You've only been a wolf for a couple of weeks, Jade. You can't seriously be considering this."

"I'm not going alone, Dom," I said and waved a hand toward Erika and her group. "They're all coming with me. They're the distraction you all need. And I'm going to give them their dead and the two that are still alive. It'll keep them busy while you guys get those kids, and if it doesn't ..."

"Dammit, Aidan!" he shouted, cutting me off and turning his flaring eyes on my mate. "This is crazy!"

"What am I supposed to do, Dom?" Aidan was shouting, too. His hands curled into fists and his face flushed with color. The muscles along his neck were straining against his skin. His inner-wolf was coming out. I could sense it in my bones, and I could smell it in the air. It was like an electrical current, the power of his scent, the raw authority of his gaze, traveling through the space between him and Dominic.

Dominic threw his hands up in the air. "You're supposed to protect your mate!"

"That's what I'm trying to do," Aidan said. "You really think I want to send her in there? Because I don't. I don't want any of you to have to do this. But the only other option I'm seeing is forcing you guys to move. Except when I think of doing that, it makes me sick. I can't walk away knowing the kind of hell this town would suffer through when we leave."

Dominic growled, and I felt a tremor of pure alpha-energy roll off of Aidan. The pack was getting nervous, fidgeting and twitching. His golden eyes sharpened their focus on Dominic, and he took a step toward him.

"Aidan," I said. I dropped Marcy's hand and walked the few steps to plant myself in front of him, trying to block Dominic from his view. I placed my hand on the swell of his pec, putting pressure on it to draw his attention to me.

"Jade." He was aggravated. I could hear it in his voice and smell the heat of it in his scent. He looked down at me, and there was a warning in his gaze, a warning I knew well.

I chose to ignore it, and I waggled a finger at him, grinning. "Don't even try that *I'm the boss* look with me. It is so not going to work, buddy. Not this time."

Aidan let out a growl, low and frustrated, and his eyes flashed brighter. I thought I was probably pushing it, but I couldn't stop myself. I dropped my hand from his chest, put it on my hip, and pursed my lips. "Did you really just growl at me in front of everyone? Not cool, Aidan."

"Jade." It was Dominic this time, and although his

voice was gentler than Aidan's, it held the same aggravation in it.

I spun on him and glowered. "Don't you 'Jade' me." My whole body was shaking, and I couldn't tell if it was from nerves or if I was just plain angry. "You're being ridiculous. I don't need to be protected. I think I've proven that to all of you a few times now."

Someone chuckled, deep and scratchy, from behind me. "I leave you guys alone for a few hours, and you've already managed to piss her off."

I turned on the voice, feeling something close to fury erupting in my belly. "I'm not pissed off," I growled. My words were followed by a gasped in a breath as I focused on who the voice belonged to. Tommy was back, and with him was Landon.

"Yes, you are," Landon said. He was smiling, and he stuffed his hands casually into the back pockets of his jeans. They sagged a little as he did it. I figured they were Aidan's; I recognized the T-shirt as Aidan's, too, and I realized he must have gone into the house and seen the mess and all the blood before coming out here. "You're all flushed pink and scrunchy-nosed. It's your mad face. I know that face."

My head started to spin, and my blood went cold. I looked from Landon to Tommy to Landon again and finally said, "You're back."

Landon suddenly looked serious and cold and wrong. He exchanged a look with Tommy and then one with Aidan. "Yep, I'm back."

CHAPTER 18

Aidan stood at the truck window, one arm resting on the door frame, as he spoke to Tommy. When I'd said that I wanted one of them to come with me, I'd meant one of the guys from the team. Someone I knew. Someone that knew me. That someone wasn't Tommy, but Tommy was who I got. I didn't exactly think he was a bad choice. He just wasn't my first.

I stood back a few feet from them. That wasn't my choice either, but they needed to talk, and Aidan had asked for a minute. I couldn't fully make out their conversation over the growing buzz of strategy talk coming from the pack, but from the small piece I did catch, I was pretty sure they were discussing the call Aidan had with his father. I didn't know the whole story on that phone call yet, but I did know that Tommy was now an official member of the Dog Mountain pack because of it.

The front lawn had become an unofficial gathering spot for the pack, which meant that there were groups scattered everywhere. Some in wolf form, others still human, but all of them were doing the same thing: getting ready for action.

"You're thinking you're not ready for this," a cool voice said from behind me.

I sighed and turned to look. Dominic. Aidan's beta, and some days he was also one of my best friends, but lately, he'd taken on the role of the biggest thorn in my side. He was watching Aidan with a critical gaze. He didn't look angry anymore, just worn, as if he'd lost a week of sleep in the last few hours. He wore jeans and a light green T-shirt, and the bare skin on his arms was raised with a layer of goosebumps from the crisp fall breeze that was blowing through the yard.

"You need to be sure, Jade," he said. "Because if you're not sure, those women will feel it. They depend on you."

Those women he was referring to were Erika and her new posse. The six of them were making their way to an SUV that was parked right behind the truck I'd be riding in. They were also the group that I'd be leading. My team.

"I am sure," I said, and I was super glad that my voice conveyed that certainty because my belly was all knotted up, and my palms were starting to sweat. The truth was I was a little scared. Okay, that was a lie. I was more than a little scared. I was terrified.

Dominic shook his head, seeing right through my lie. "Your scent gives you away, honey," he said quietly. He took a step toward me, and his blue eyes were steady on mine. "Run me through it. Every step, okay?"

I hoped I didn't look as crazy relieved as I felt. Pain in the ass or not, Dominic knew exactly what to do to help. He always had. Sometimes I thought he even knew me better than I knew myself.

I pulled in a deep breath. "Yeah, okay," I said and pasted on what was meant to be my *game face* and nodded. "My team is up front. The two cougars who are still alive are riding with the girls to make my offer more believable. We stop at one of the two checkpoints on the way to the hunt camp, where Landon left one of the wolves that went with him. The other five teams will stop at the second checkpoint before fanning out and surrounding the camp. The girls will keep the cougars busy while I jump out at the checkpoint to make sure there's been no movement from the hunting camp."

I hesitated and gritted my teeth. The plan was good. I knew that, but putting my females right in the thick of things ... It wasn't sitting well with me. The truth? My biggest fear about this whole thing was that I wouldn't be able to keep those women safe.

"Good," Dominic said, his eyes still holding steady. "What's next?"

"We drive into the center of their camp," I said and swallowed hard. "The girls are going to park off to the side and back a bit. Tommy and I get out first. I explain that we want the feud to be over. I tell them that my dad was right and that we should be allies, not rivals. I give them their dead, and then I give them the girls and the cougars as a peace offering."

God, what if I fail them? My hands were starting to tremble, and I quickly jammed them into my pockets, trying to hide the shakes, but I didn't think I did it fast enough.

Dominic's gaze flicked down to my hands and then back up to my eyes. "By the time you're done giving them over, the kids will be in the SUV and gone, and the rest of us will move in." His voice sounded normal and steady, and I wondered how he did that, considering what we were about to do. Even his expression was calm. "We've got this, Jade."

I wanted to agree with him because I really did believe that this could work. We doubled the werecougars in numbers. We had a strong group. I really thought that it was possible to win this fight. But instead of agreeing, I asked, "Do you think it's a bad idea to go without assigning a head enforcer to lead the attack?" I knew it was something Dominic had been worried about, and I thought Aidan was, too. The rest of the pack had been divided into five groups, which were to be led by Beck, Craig, Landon, Mark, and Aidan. It was Aidan's idea of a quick fix to choosing a head enforcer. Instead, he made them all leaders to their own teams, hoping it would keep them from undermining each other and pulling the pack in a bunch of different directions while we were out there.

Dominic thought about it for a second. "I think what he's done, splitting them up like this, will work." He folded his arms across his chest. "But, Jade, when this is over, you better make sure he deals with it. A team without a head is like a pack without a mated alpha pair. Things start to fall apart."

"I will," I said, with a bob of my head, and I meant it. The last thing we needed was for things to fall apart with the pack again. We'd just pulled them all back together.

Dominic nodded. He looked away, hesitated for a second, and then reached out for me. He pulled me into a hug and held on tight for a long moment before letting go. "You're going to do great," he said, and then he turned and went back to the group he'd been assigned to.

I waited tensely for Aidan to finish up. It felt like time stopped for about a year while I stood there, watching the muscles in his neck and jaw tense and release only to tense up again.

"Hey, Jade," Marcy called, and I glanced up. She shook her hand in an awkward wave as she edged past a group of wolves, who were pacing around restlessly, then jogged over to me.

"Hey," I said. "Where's Trevor?"

She rolled her eyes and pointed off to her left, where a group of four wolves was gathered. "He's over there with Beck, and Beck thinks I'm a distraction, so he made his group shift."

I snorted out a laugh. "You? A distraction? Never."

Marcy didn't laugh, not even a little. She swiveled on her heels to look at me fully. "You know Mom's inside trying to scrub the blood out of the carpet, right?"

"Yeah," I said and looked back at the house. "She tried to convince us to let her come with us. She says she needs to be a part of this. When Aidan told her no, she started to clean, telling us that she had to do something." I felt an angry heat building in my face, and my stomach started to twist in knots again. "She's blaming herself, Mac. She thinks she should have seen through Dad. She thinks she should have stopped him. I tried to get her to stop, and she whipped a scrub brush at me, yelling at me to get out."

"Oh," she said. She started chewing on her lip so hard it was almost white, and then suddenly, she threw herself at me hard enough that I rocked back a step before I caught my balance. I hugged her back, though, as tightly as I could. She smelled of Trevor, musk and a hint of spice, and a layer of vanilla body spray, with a light undertone of bitter anxiety. "Be safe, Jade," she whispered. "Don't do anything impulsive."

I didn't say anything. I really didn't think there was anything I could say to make her feel better. So I just continued to squeeze her tightly, hoping that it would give her some kind of reassurance.

A throat cleared, and we slowly, reluctantly, pulled apart. Aidan. He looked from me to Marcy as if he weren't quite sure if he should be interrupting us just yet. "I've got Tommy caught up," he said. His voice was gentle, and his gaze, patient. His lips curved very slightly. "He's ready to go ... whenever you are."

"I'm just going to ..." Marcy backed up a couple steps and stopped. She looked utterly lost for a second, but then her eyes brightened a little. "I'm going to go finish the last-minute details for tonight and pick up Jared's remains." Her voice sounded faint and torn, and she started blinking fast, but she looked a little less lost as if she'd found a purpose.

"Thank you, Mac," Aidan said gently. "That would be a really big help."

She just shrugged as if to say it was no big deal. But it was. When we got back, it would be good for the guys, for the whole pack, to put Jared to rest because we would be coming back. And I thought she knew that, too.

"Just bring them all home, okay?" she said.

"We will, Mac," he said. "Promise." And I hoped it wasn't a promise that would end up broken.

Marcy nodded and gave us a weak smile before she turned and headed for Trevor's truck. She waved to us from the driver's seat before starting it up, and then she pulled out of the driveway.

Aidan stepped in behind me, and his arms went around my waist. "Time to go," he said roughly. He gave me a hug that was too quick and not nearly tight enough. "Listen to Tommy. Trust him, okay? He'll watch out for you until I can get back to your side."

"I don't like splitting up," I blurted, turning around to look at him. "I really wish we didn't have to do that."

Aidan's face went still and a little too tight, and I realized that he didn't like it either. "Don't think of it as splitting up," he said. "I'm going to be right there with you. We're going to get through this. I promise you, we will. And when we do, we're going to do something boring. Really, really boring."

"You know," I said, fighting to hide the tension in my voice because the last thing he needed was to worry about me when I needed him to worry about everyone else. I even smiled a little. "Boring actually sounds like fun right about now."

He chuckled, and a flash of what looked like relief passed across his face. He smoothed my hair back and leaned down to kiss me. The kiss was soft and sweet, and it felt so much like a goodbye that it made my chest ache and my throat close up. I clung onto him and dug a hand into his hair, holding his mouth to mine. I didn't want him to stop. I didn't want to lose the connection. I didn't want goodbye.

And it worked for a second, but only a second. He took my wrist gently in his hand and pulled it from his hair, and then he pulled back. "This isn't goodbye, sweetheart," he said as if reading my thought. "I'm going to be right behind you. It's going to work out." He leaned in close then, so close that his lips brushed my ear, and he whispered gruffly, "I'll see you soon, sweetheart. Love you."

And then I stepped back, and I felt all jittery and nervous, but I tried really hard to hide it. I even thought I succeeded — sort of. I shoved back my fear, took a deep breath, and I gave him the best game face I could muster up and said, "Love you, too." And with another quick hug, I turned away from him and walked over to the waiting SUV to get my girls ready.

CHAPTER 19

AIDAN

I was smiling. It was a big smile, and I probably looked goofy, but I couldn't stop it. For a second there, I thought Jade was going to crack. The way she'd kissed me. The way she'd clung onto me. It felt scared and uncertain.

I didn't blame her for that. She hadn't been a werewolf long. She was still growing into it, learning her strengths, figuring out who she was within the pack, but feeling her hesitation made me nervous. Maybe she wasn't ready for this. Maybe she wasn't ready to clean out her father's pack.

But then she walked away. And she seemed okay. Confident. Ready.

It was a tremendous relief.

She was standing at the SUV giving the girls a pep talk, and unlike Beck's pep talk to the pack earlier, this one was actually peppy. The women were relaxing. They were even smiling a little.

Erika and Laura broke off from the group and jogged over to the garage. They lifted the door halfway and ducked underneath, and a moment later, I heard their muffled voices as they set the plan in motion.

They were ready.

I glanced back at the SUV. Jade was looking back at me with an intense, warm focus, and for a second, I felt as if I were the only person there. She had a way of doing that when she looked at me. She made me feel as if I were the only thing she saw. As if I were the only thing worth seeing. It was kind of surreal. Even when we were about to attack — and kill — a pack of werecougars, she could still make me feel as if I were *it* for her just by a look. As if I were her home.

The moment didn't last long. Jade gave me an eye roll and then a little chin jerk. The girls had, I noticed, piled into the SUV. Low growls filled my ears, and a throaty, seductive laugh came from behind me. I knew the laugh. I'd heard it before. Erika.

But those growls ... they needed to stop. I spun on the pack, most of who were already in wolf form. "Enough," I said. I let my scent gather and roll off me quickly in a warning, and the growls died down.

"Come on," Erika said, tugging on the tall one's hand. "I've got some friends waiting to meet you in that SUV over there." She batted her lashes and giggled. "I think you'll like them."

The four of them made their way across the yard, and I was a little surprised to see that the cougars didn't seem at all worried about the wolves scattered around them.

Stupid, I thought and wondered how they'd managed to hide from us for so long. But I figured I knew the answer to that. Jeff. He was obviously the brains behind the whole *uniting shifters* thing, and I bet he was the one who'd kept them on the move, jumping locations and hiding in hunting camps. He was also the one who fed their sick addiction.

My inner-wolf paced restlessly within me, just itching for the moment he could tear into these monsters, and as they got closer, it was a struggle to keep him and my steady gaze in place. "Sorry for the misunderstanding, guys," I said. "Hope there are no hard feelings."

"Not a problem," the short one said, wrapping an arm around Laura. "She'll make up for it." He looked around then, eyeing the wolves curiously. "You guys going somewhere?"

I shrugged. "Nowhere, really. Just a run. Wanted to see the girls off before we left. Make sure they didn't give you any problems."

"Why would we give them problems?" Laura asked, mystified. "We volunteered, and honestly, I can't wait to meet them all." Her scent was screaming excitement, mixed with a little touch of nerves. And the cougars were responding to it, although it wasn't in the way they probably should have been. They were breathing it in, nostrils flaring, their scents matching hers. It was perfect. She mimicked Erika's throaty laugh and smiled demurely.

Yep, definitely stupid.

I chuckled. "Glad to hear it." I glanced at the tall one and smiled a little. "You take care of my girls, now."

"We will," he said, and with that, Erika and Laura tugged them over to the waiting vehicle.

I didn't watch them go. I couldn't. My inner-wolf was pushing to get out, frantic to stop them, and I knew that if I tried to watch, I'd wind up doing something stupid that would ruin everything. So I looked to Jade, and she gave me that warm *you're my home* gaze. She smiled. I smiled. She waved. I waved.

And then she jumped into the truck, and it growled to life, and as it started to inch forward, I turned back to my pack.

"Let's get this done," I said and yanked my shirt off. I pulled the button and zipper open on my jeans, letting them fall. Adrenaline hit me hard and fast, the rush of the shift pulsed through my veins, and I let my inner-wolf spring free.

JADE

The drive would have been so much better if Tommy actually talked.

Tommy wouldn't talk to me. I tried everything. I asked about Chris. His response was two words: *gone home*. I tried to go over the plan, he said three words: *you know it*. I even tried to talk about the weather, and all I got to that was a grunt.

I didn't think it was me exactly. After about five minutes into the drive, I decided that he just really wasn't a talker. The problem with not talking, though, was that the silence was killing me. It was giving me way too much time in my head, imagining all the ways that Aidan or Dominic or Beck or Landon or Erika or Laura or any of the pack members, for that matter, could die.

A week ago, I probably would have laughed off the thought of one of us dying by someone outside of our pack as a bad joke, but then Jared died, and even though it was Aidan who killed him, it made us all a little less invincible to me. Because if an enforcer could die, any of us could.

I had to admit, even though I was crazy nervous, it had been a pretty smooth drive so far. We passed the checkpoint without a hitch, and the girls kept the werecougars occupied during the short stop. Things were going exactly to plan. I wasn't really sure what I'd expected, but since we'd accumulated five dead bodies in the last twelve hours and they were in the back of the truck, smooth and uneventful, wasn't it.

I was fidgeting. Wiggling in my seat. Playing with the window. Anything to try to distract myself. And when Tommy gave me a five-minute warning, I thought my heart was about ready to give out on me. Then, when the hunting camp came into view, I stopped breathing until my lungs were burning, and I was gasping for breath.

"You've got to relax, Jade," he said as he maneuvered the truck slowly into the small, narrow driveway. He sounded bitter, annoyed, and he cut me a quick look. "I'm not going to let anything happen to you."

"I'm not worried about me," I said. My tone was just short of a shout. "I'm worried about those kids and the girls in the car and the pack. I'm freaked out that I'm going to fail them again. I don't care about my safety. I care about them!"

Tommy put the truck in park and shut it off. He looked at me then, a thorough, invasive look that felt as if he saw right through me. He narrowed his eyes and pulled in a few deep breaths, and then, he nodded as if he'd found whatever he'd been looking for. "I won't let you fail them." And he sounded completely sure of that.

I nodded because, well, I didn't have a clue what to say to that. He must have accepted my nod as some kind of agreement because he looked away. He did a quick, thorough sweep of the area, and for a long moment, there was nothing. No movement, no people. Nothing.

The cabin, a rustic-looking log structure, looked empty — almost deserted. If it weren't for the fire pit blazing and what looked like a pig rotating within the flames, I would have sworn no one was here.

The yard, if you could even call it that, was small. A clothesline was strung up, running from one side of the cabin to the nearest oak, filled with clothing and a few picnic tables that looked set for a meal.

I glanced behind us and spotted the girls parked at the bottom of the driveway, off to the side. Erika was at the wheel, scanning the dense forest beside them, and I wondered, briefly, what the others were doing to keep the cougars distracted and in the SUV. But then I felt like throwing up, and I thought it was probably best not to think about it.

They know what they're doing. They wanted to do this. It was their idea.

"Cabin," Tommy said. "The curtains just moved."

I swiveled back around. He was right. The curtain twitched, parting just a little in the center, and then fluttered closed again.

"What do you think they're waiting for?" I whispered. I wasn't sure why I was whispering, but that's how my voice had chosen to work.

"Probably waiting for us to leave."

"Then we should get out," I said and reached for the door handle.

Tommy's hand clamped down onto my shoulder and held me back. "Not yet," he said. "Aidan's team is to your right. I spotted Beck up ahead and Craig to his left. No sign of Mark and Landon yet. We should wait until they come out. Buy the others some more time to get into place."

I snapped my gaze to the right and peered out the window, searching for Aidan. It took a long second before I spotted a flash of his black coat amongst the trees and foliage, but when I spotted him, my anxiety started to melt, and I felt the game face I'd been faking for the last hour fix into place. My inner-wolf began to stir, urging me to get moving, and I looked back at Tommy. "The girls ..."

"They're fine," he interrupted. "There are six of

them in that SUV. Only two cougars in there with them. You're not going to let them down. Trust me, we need to wait."

My inner-wolf didn't like that response. She reared up, clawing and pressing against my chest. She didn't want to wait. She wanted to get outside, get things moving, and get back to her mate, and it took a whole lot of effort to force her back into the pit of my stomach. But I managed and gave him a gasping nod. "Okay. We wait." Because it was probably the smart thing to do, right? We didn't even know if all the werecougars were actually in that cabin.

It took another seven long minutes for more movement from the cabin, but this time it wasn't twitching curtains. The door swung open, and a group of men filed out.

And then there were people all around us, circling the truck and the SUV behind us. It felt like a heck of a lot more than fourteen, but with a quick count, I found out it was fourteen exactly.

Someone stopped next to the truck and peered in the window. It was a lean, medium-height man. He was good-looking, too, maybe twenty-five years old, with dusty-blond hair and startlingly bright green eyes. He had a surprisingly friendly smile, considering we had five of his pack members dead in the bed of the truck. And I had no doubt that he knew they were there even though they were covered up in blankets and tarps. I could smell them, and I had all the windows closed. He was even wearing a faded T-shirt with a big yellow smiley face on it.

Not really what I was expecting.

He waved and tapped on the window. His smile grew, and if it weren't for the overwhelming smell of cougar, I would have thought we were in the wrong place.

I pulled in a deep breath as I reached for the door handle, and again, Tommy grabbed my shoulder and stopped me. I sent him a sharp look, and I swore I saw amusement in his eyes. "Slow down," he said. "Just roll down the window and tell him why we're here."

I shrugged off his hand and pressed the bottom for the window to slide down. As soon as it was open a few inches, the man asked, "You lost?" He had a nice voice. Deep and smooth.

That probably shouldn't have thrown me off, but mixed with his friendly smile and the big smiley face on his shirt, it did for a second. And I found myself genuinely smiling back as I said, "Nope. I'm Jade Shaw, and I'm looking for my dad."

CHAPTER 20

AIDAN

Being stealthy in the fall was seriously not an easy task. Dried-up leaves seemed to be everywhere, and each time one of my wolves stepped on them, the crunching sound was deafening. And with most of the leaves now on the ground, the forest felt open, as if there were no coverage, nothing to keep us hidden.

It sucked.

I circled my group along the west side of the cabin, moving in slowly, creeping as quietly as we could. The place felt almost ... abandoned. Through the trees, the yard looked empty. And it was quiet. Too quiet. The only sounds seemed to be coming from us as we moved into place.

But I could smell them. The cougars were here. That bitter lemon and birch bark scent were thick in the air. Suffocating.

There were two barbed wire cages at the side of the building. They were empty, but seeing them, knowing what they were used for, and knowing that I'd sent some of my females here, tied my stomach into knots.

Don't think about it. They'll never get close enough to see the inside of those cages.

Jade and Tommy were already in place. I could just make out their outlines within the truck from my position. It was parked in the narrow-looking driveway, probably twenty feet from the cabin, and behind it, as close to the tree line as it could get, was the SUV.

Up ahead, I spotted one of the other groups, waiting. Beck's light gray coat stood out, in stark contrast with the forest's browns and reds and oranges. I hadn't spotted any of the other groups yet, but I could hear them. A twig snapping. Dry leaves crumbling. They were here, closing in and surrounding the yard.

Minutes passed, and everything was still. It was as if the entire forest were holding its breath. Waiting. Watching.

It seemed quiet, very, very quiet.

Jade and Tommy still hadn't gotten out of the truck. I figured they were probably seeing something that I couldn't. Something that held them inside. Something that kept them waiting.

They had to be in the cabin, I thought. It was the only place for them to hide. If they were in the woods, we would have come across them. We would have spotted them. With so many of us surrounding the camp, I was sure of that.

A dark, weighted feeling gathered in the pit of my stomach, and I fought the urge to growl. If they were in the cabin, the kids would be, too, and I wasn't entirely sure how to get in, grab them, and get them out without drawing attention. I'd been counting on them being out in the open and using Jade and the girls as a distraction to snatch them away.

Another minute passed. And another. And then, the door on the hunting camp banged open, and a group of men stalked out. They fanned out around the truck as another stream of them spilled out of the building, moving toward the SUV.

I kept my eyes peeled, searching for the children. Waiting for them. But things were happening. People were gathering around both of the vehicles. Talking. Arguing.

Jade, Tommy, the girls, they hadn't gotten out yet, but still, I didn't like what I was seeing, and I could tell that the group with me didn't like it either.

A man, not much older than me, approached the truck, and Jade rolled her window down. She said something to him, something that made him stiffen, and his hands curled into fists.

Everyone else froze. The talking, the arguing, all of it just stopped.

Dominic nudged my side and whimpered quietly. He swung his head toward the truck. I knew exactly what he wanted. Damn, we all wanted to move in, but the kids ...

I thought I heard something, and I froze. So did the others. And a half-second later, I knew I heard something. A light, almost delicate, thump, and then another, and then another, all coming from right behind us.

I exchanged a quick look with the others, and as a unit, we pivoted, teeth bared and deadly growls rolling out.

JADE

Dead silence. My stomach lurched. Everyone outside was frozen, staring at me. And that infectious, friendly smile on the guy standing at my window was changing into something not so friendly — something dark.

He leaned in closer to the window, and the look

on his face was hard. The door latch popped, and he yanked it open. "Get out."

I glanced at Tommy. He gave me a small nod, and I turned back to the guy. "Um, yeah, sure. Is my dad here?"

"Depends," he said and gestured for me to get out.

"Depends on what?" I asked as I swung my legs around to hop down. I guessed I wasn't moving fast enough for him because his hands circled my waist, and he lifted me out of the truck.

Tommy growled. It was low and rough and fierce, and by the time my feet hit the ground, he was already out of the truck and beside me. His hand closed around my wrist, yanking me away from the smiley face guy.

"Tommy, I'm good," I said, attempting, and failing, to shake off his too-tight grip. "Seriously, let go. I'm good."

He didn't let go but did loosen up a little. They stared off for an angry moment, and I was uncomfortably aware of the werecougars moving in around us. I also thought I heard a whimper coming from where I'd spotted Aidan, but it was hard to be sure. My blood was pumping fast, my heart, pounding in my ears, and my head was starting to get a little fuzzy from the continuous stream of adrenaline that flooded through me as my inner-wolf fought to come out.

"I want to see my dad," I said and tried to sound demanding. It probably would have been more convincing if I wasn't so frazzled. "He told me to come here if I changed my mind."

The guy raised his eyebrows, and his green eyes sparkled with cold amusement. "I bet he told you to kill some of my pack mates and bring them with you, too."

"No," I said shortly, staring first at him, then at

Tommy. We exchanged a look that I didn't understand, and I shrugged helplessly. "Look, it was either them or me." I sighed, looking back to the guy. "I didn't have much of a choice. But I figured you guys might want to bury them or something, so I brought them."

"How considerate of you."

I shook my head in response and found myself looking at Tommy again. He turned his head and looked at me briefly, and I hoped he caught the huge *what the hell?* in my expression. But if he did, he ignored it.

The men were still inching in, and I eased back, shaking off Tommy's hand. No one else was talking. Not even a whispered sound had passed amongst the werecougars since I'd mentioned my name.

The guy, who I assumed was the official werecougars' spokesperson, let out an assumed chuckle. He looked like he was about to say something I wasn't going to like but froze when Tommy grumbled, "She brought a peace offering."

Tommy glanced at the SUV and waved a hand, then leaned back against the truck, folding his arms over his chest, and watched the proceedings with what looked like detached interest.

Erika was the first to come out. She didn't hesitate, strutting toward us, chin high and shoulders back. Laura was next, and attached to her was one of the werecougars. She was giggling and smiling, and if I hadn't known any better, I would have sworn she was actually into the guy.

One by one, my females came forward, smiling, offering little waves. They pushed their way into the circle of men surrounding me and Tommy and the truck. But the two werecougars we'd brought back didn't follow them. They paused and blended into the circle around us.

And still not a sound from the others. They were detached. Quiet. Watching. It was … confusing. I licked my lips.

I was suddenly hoping that Aidan had found the children. That any second now, the SUV would speed away, and my pack would descend on the werecougars, because this quietness … I didn't know what to make of it. It was worse than seeing aggression. At least I would have known how to deal with that.

I turned to face the smiley face guy, who was looking at me thoughtfully. "What did you change your mind about?"

I blinked and shook my head, thrown off for a second. "Oh," I said and glanced back at the women. "I'm ready to make the deal. I'm giving you some of our females. In exchange, you all stay the hell out of Dog Mountain."

"Thought they were the peace offering," he said, eyeing me carefully, if not critically.

"Some are," I said and shrugged. "But you don't get them all until I get confirmation from my dad that the deal is still on the table."

He cocked his head slightly, shifting his gaze toward the woods, and then he leaned in close to my ear and said, "Did you hear that?"

I did. It had sounded like a strangled whimper. And a snarl. A vicious snarl that ended in a surprised yip. More whimpering, some growls. Cracks and creaks and crunches. Leaves crumbling. Twigs snapping. The sounds came from every direction. But I looked at him blankly and asked, "Did I hear what?

He was smiling again. The nice one. The infectious one. And it made my blood run cold as ice. "That, Jade

Shaw," he said, and his smile grew wider, "is the sound of your pack dying."

CHAPTER 21

AIDAN

My father wasn't a thinker. He had a problem; he fixed it — usually with unnecessary violence — but he didn't think about it. He acted. And as much as that had bothered me in the past, right then, I was seeing the wisdom in his impulsiveness.

I'd taken after my mom, though. I liked to have a plan. I liked to know what I was getting into. But the thing with having a plan was that you think you've got the situation covered. You lose that rush that keeps you on your toes. You miss things. You get cocky. And sometimes planning and strategizing and overthinking gets you to a place that you can't see a way out of.

And right then, I was in that place.

The wolves around me looked a little confused about what they were supposed to do. Dominic was crouched down next to me, a continuous growl rumbling from his chest. Cougars were falling from the trees surrounding us.

With a sharp feeling of alarm, I remembered what Jade had said about the claw marks in the trees. She'd known. She'd told us. We'd even discussed it. And in all the planning and scouting, no one had paid attention to it.

They'd known we were coming. *Dammit!* They'd probably been watching us the whole time while we scouted out the location. I should have known they'd have some kind of security in place. Jeff wasn't stupid. I should have ...

No. I wouldn't think about that. I couldn't think about that. Because if I thought about it, I'd realize that they'd been hiding in the trees all this time and that we were probably staggeringly outnumbered. And if I thought about that, if I let those numbers get into my head, I'd start to worry about Jade and my females who were trapped and surrounded and alone in there.

The wolves in my group were pacing, circling, dodging, growling. Waiting for the signal. Waiting for my command that the fight was on.

I let instinct take over. I channeled my scent and gave the signal to attack — to fight.

And they did.

One of the wolves let out a full-out vicious snarl, and then everything happened quickly. Wolves moved, cougars pounced, and all I could do was hope that the kids were tucked safely in that cabin and they stayed put.

More whisper-soft thumps. Wolves and cougars cried and screamed and snarled. It came from everywhere, all at once.

Something dropped beside me, and I pivoted, crouching down, and bared my teeth. I felt an ugly mix of anger and hatred churn within my belly, and I growled at the beast as it stalked toward me, with all the confident grace of a house cat.

It hissed. I snarled. It circled right. I circled left. I launched forward, and it slipped back. Playing with me.

My blood was pumping hard and fast, and furious energy twisted and curled throughout my body. The sounds of flesh ripping, tearing, pulling, pounded through my ears. Hisses tormented me, a growl filled my chest. I could almost taste the blood that was being spilled all around me.

The cat lunged for me, a blur of beige in the colorful forest, and I twisted and dropped to my belly.

The cougar missed me, landing with a hard thump to my right — not far away, but not on top of me, either. He let out a wail and spun around. His eyes were wild, and his lips were curled back.

I slammed into its body, hard enough to knock it down to the ground. I didn't have long once he was down; the shock of the impact wouldn't keep the beast at bay for more than a second or two. It flinched, trying to shimmy and roll back to its feet, but I didn't let him. I pushed off, landing on top of him, and bit down hard. In a second, the cougar went limp, falling face down into the dirt.

I shot up quickly, scanning the area around us. More wolves were joining our group, and seeing them sent a surge of hope through me. If they were joining, maybe, *maybe*, there hadn't been that many cougars in the trees.

A high-pitched screech came from my left, and I spun toward the sound. A bird — a large, black bird — dove at me. His talons sunk into my flesh near my neck, and I snarled, tossing my body to the ground and shaking him loose.

The bird let go and then dove at me again, but as it lowered, it started to change. It got bigger. Fur replaced the feathers. Paws replaced the talons, and when the beast hit the ground, its wings seemingly melted away, and I was suddenly standing face to face with a cougar.

Jeff. I knew he wouldn't have run.

I growled, curling my lips back and baring my teeth. He tensed, bracing himself, as I crouched slightly, leveling my eyes with his. He didn't make a sound. No hisses, no snarls. His eyes looked as if they were laughing, full of humor, and I found myself growling again.

It's another game, I told myself. *He's playing with me.* I was sure of it, but his calmness made me uneasy, and for a moment, it kept me rooted in place.

A loud, pain-filled howl erupted from my right, and my eyes darted to the side, just a quick look. I spotted Dominic, falling, tumbling, down. He tried to get up, but he wasn't quick enough. A cougar landed squarely on his back, pinning him.

My heart twisted inside my chest. I glanced back to Jeff, but he was ... gone. Melted into to chaos that surrounded me.

Another agonized howl tore from my best friend, and I launched myself toward Dominic.

A flash of pain rushed through my back leg. I stumbled, fell, and as I started to roll, I felt something sharp dig into my leg. It was crippling. It felt like my leg was being ripped off. I snarled. More pain. Sharp, hot pain.

The cougar tore into Dominic's back, and my hope sputtered and flickered and died.

JADE

I kept my breathing under control, mainly by sternly telling myself that I had to remain completely together. The wolves around the hunting camp weren't my problem. They each had a leader. They each had someone watching their back. My problem, my responsibility, was the women with Tommy and me. I had my breathing more or less managed by the time I spun from the guy, who was still smiling, a far too friendly smile, and I was able to say, "Shift," without making it sound like I was panicking at all.

But the truth was, I was a little panicked.

"I wouldn't do that," a man said and pulled a handgun from the waist of his jeans. He leveled it on me.

That was, for some reason, kind of a shock because, well, he was a werecougar. He could shift and kill me. The gun just seemed really ... unnecessary. "You're kidding me, right?" I blinked. "You're pulling a gun on me?"

"It made them stop, didn't it?" the man with the gun said, his voice sounding antagonistic and a touch condescending.

I could smell Aidan. His alpha scent, that sweet green scent, was rising up around me. Commanding our wolves. The sounds were getting louder. Snarls and painful whimpers. They were in trouble. They hadn't reached the kids. The plan was falling apart.

My entire body was alive with feeling. My pulse was pounding in my ears and temples, and wrists. My skin was buzzing and tingling. Warmth spread from tip to toe, adrenaline chasing through my system.

I took a step and more guns, small handguns, appeared. I laughed once. "Am I really that scary to you all?" I asked and laughed again. "You guys better hope you have perfect aim if you plan on using them."

Smiley face guy chuckled and moved in close to me, so close that I could feel his warm breath puffing against my face. I held his eyes, refusing to flinch. His vibrant eyes were smiling, taunting, cruel, and confident.

He was poison hidden behind pretty eyes and a killer smile.

"I love that sound," he said, and he looked almost ... wistful. His nostrils flared wide as he hauled a full breath into his lungs. "And that smell. I bet some of it's coming from your mate." He licked his lips. "And some from that friend of yours."

He could have been right, but my nose was telling me that the blood wasn't just from wolves, and well, I wasn't even going to consider the possibility that some of that blood could be Aidan's. I just couldn't.

I forced a snide smile. "Nope. Smells like cougar blood to me. I've killed a few of those recently. I know that smell."

He slapped me in the face so quickly that I hadn't even seen him move until he connected with my cheek and sent me staggering back. My whole body quivered, and a growl ripped from my throat. Bones started to break. My ankle went first, then my elbow. My face was shifting, my teeth lengthening. All around me, I could hear my pack fighting, snarling, and falling. Okay, maybe I couldn't hear them actually falling, but my brain was conjuring up a pretty vivid image of wolves lying motionless on the ground, blood pooling, cougars watching ...

I hardly noticed the guns anymore. Somewhere in the back of my mind, I knew they were still trained on me, but I didn't care. I let my scent gather, and I was about to force my wolves to shift when Tommy said, "Jade, don't."

He was still leaning back against the truck, and I had to admit, it shocked me. At some point, he'd raised his hands, carefully holding his palms out in surrender. But those hands had claws now, and coarse, dark hair layered the tops. His face was like stone, set in a murderous expression, and his eyes blazed gold.

The man — Mr. Smiley Spokesperson — barked out a laugh. "Yeah," he agreed. "Don't." He didn't seem to notice how close Tommy and I were to shifting, or maybe he just didn't think that any of us were a threat at all. He actually turned his back on us and looked at my girls, who I noticed, were just barely holding onto their skin.

Underestimating us was a stupid, stupid mistake.

My breath caught. A string of pops and snaps rang through the air. Fabric tore. Flares of heat shot through my limbs.

The guns opened fire. Shots rattled against the truck, and the windshield exploded into cracks. But by the time the first searing bullet grazed my skin, the guy who turned his back on me was already falling.

CHAPTER 22

AIDAN

I could only stare. The body lying not even ten feet from me — Dominic's — didn't look to be alive. He wasn't moving. He didn't look as if he were breathing. The rusty-brown wolf had fallen to his side. His muzzle was open slightly, his eyes were shut, and his legs and paws looked loose and relaxed. He almost looked as if he were sleeping, and if it weren't for the chunk of flesh and fur missing from in between his shoulders and the blood soaking into the ground around him, I might have thought he was.

Except he wasn't moving at all. Not even a quiver of his chest from a shallow breath.

I squeezed my eyes shut. This couldn't be happening. He couldn't be dead. He just couldn't be. But when I opened my eyes, Dominic was still on the ground, and he still wasn't moving.

I hadn't felt scared during the attack. Not really. Not until now. I'd been focused, determined. But now ... now I was terrified. My mouth was dry, shriveled up, and so was my throat. Dominic was my friend, the best friend I had in Dog Mountain, and he was ... I let out a painful whimper.

Somewhere in the back of my mind, I was aware that gunshots were still ringing out, but I couldn't pull my eyes away from him.

Seeing him so still, hurt worse than anything I'd ever felt before. I should have saved him. I was his alpha, his friend. I should have gotten to him. I should have ...

Jade.

My heart started to pound, and my chest constricted with dread. She was still in there with her team. I needed to get to them. Get them away from the bullets. I needed to get them out of there.

I tore my eyes from my best friend, my beta, and surveyed my surroundings with a quick, swiping scan. I was surrounded by death. Cougars and wolves. Bodies and blood. My wolves were everywhere. Some lying on the ground, injured, some still fighting.

I tried to stand up, but the pain in my back legs seized me up tight. They were broken. I could feel the bones grinding as I tried to get to my feet again, and when I glanced down and saw how not straight they were, I winced. They were a mess, bones snapped, and flesh was torn up.

I growled. I was useless to Jade, to my pack, like this. I needed to shift and let my broken bones reset and mend.

I wasn't sure what had happened. One second I had one of those bastards trying to gnaw off my legs, and the next, there'd been a series of cracks that sounded a heck of a lot like gunfire, and the cougar had let me go.

It felt like it took hours for my body to change forms, but I was sure it was just a few seconds. My inner-wolf fought against the shift, struggling to stay in control. All he wanted was to fight, kill, and claim back what was ours.

Each broken bone in my legs burned as it snapped again and reset itself, and by the time I finished, I was covered in a thin sheen of sweat, and my breath was strained and labored.

Another round of sharp, loud cracks came from the direction of the hunting camp. Panic welled up inside me. I pushed up to my feet, and a twinge of pain shot through me as I put my weight on my legs, but it wasn't unbearable. My legs were moving before my brain could catch up, and I was running toward the edge of the forest.

I saw her — my mate — through the trees. She was in wolf form, just lying there on the ground. A man — it was the man who'd been at her window — was standing over her. The shoulder of his T-shirt was drenched in blood, I noticed, as he bent down beside her. He reached out to touch her midnight black coat, and I felt the wildest, strongest impulse to rip him apart from limb to limb. I could visualize it, and it was alarming and so very satisfying.

And then Jade moved. Her skin started to crawl, and she began to shake. She was shifting, I realized, and I felt myself run faster.

I reached the edge of the tree line just as a set of arms wrapped around my chest, hauling me back. "Aidan, stop!" Mark said.

"Let go of me," I commanded, my tone firm, direct, and full of fury. My imprint was blazing, and my scent, thick in the air. "Let go!"

"They won't hurt her," he growled. His eyes were red and blurred with exhaustion. "They need her. Stop and think, Aidan!"

Mark started to pant, and his arms were weakening. I twisted and yanked my body free of his grasp, and as I did, Craig darted in front of me and shoved me back a step. "You can't help her, or any of us, if you're dead." He was straining, too. Fighting to stay strong and on his feet under the force of my alpha scent. "Look around!" he shouted, panicked and flailing his arm to point behind me. "They need you more than she does right now!"

When I only growled, Craig shoved me again. He puffed out his chest, squaring off with me, and pointed behind me again. I wasn't sure what he wanted me to see. I wasn't sure if I even cared. In the back of my mind, I knew that if the enforcers thought Jade was in real danger, they wouldn't be stopping me. They'd be killing anything that stood in their way to get to my girl. She was one of theirs just as much as she was mine.

My nostrils flared, and every muscle in my body was strung tight as I did a slow circle, looking to where he'd pointed.

There was movement all around me. Whimpering. Heavy breathing. Disturbed leaves crunched and crumbled. *My wolves.* They were stirring, limping to their feet, healing.

And the cougars that had been hiding in the trees were dead. All of them.

Someone coughed, a hacking, painful cough, and the sound made my breath hitch. My gaze snapped to Dominic. Beck was standing by him now, his bloodstained muzzle nudging at Dominic's shoulder.

A strangled sound worked up through my chest, and my eyes started to burn. Dominic wasn't dead. I blinked and then blinked again. He'd managed to shift and pull himself into a sitting position, resting his head in his hands. He was breathing hard, sweating, shaking, coughing. But he wasn't dead.

Silence fell. Complete silence. The gunshots stopped. The screams silenced. I swallowed hard and looked back to where Jade was lying to see the man drape a blanket over her. And the other females were being lifted and carried to the cabin. They weren't being hurt. The men looked as though they were being careful, gentle even, now that my females were unconscious.

And everything snapped into hot, sharp clarity.

Uniting the shifters. Jeff didn't want us dead. He wanted us to join him. But he wouldn't be that stupid, right? Keeping the girls, even if they were wounded, was dangerous. They'd heal, and he had to know that we'd come for them.

Craig's hand fell on my shoulder and tightened. "We've got to move."

"What?" I asked and turned my head to look at him. I felt rage, so hot, so pure, it felt like I was burning from the inside out, and it felt terrifyingly good. "We're not going anywhere without our females."

He saw my rage. His hand skittered away from my shoulder, and his eyes dropped to the ground. "They can't fight," he said. "Most of them are struggling to walk. We need to fall back."

"I'm not leaving her." My voice was growled, and my eyes flared. "We're not leaving any of them, the girls or the kids."

Craig didn't say anything, but he hadn't moved out of my way, either. I felt my face go red, and the muscles in my clenched jaw fluttered. My scent ramped up, my imprint blazed.

"Aidan," Mark said in a soft, tentative voice from behind me. "Look at them. They've got to heal. We can't help the kids if we're dead, and you need to trust Jade to do her job. She'll keep those girls safe."

I didn't turn. I couldn't. I knew what I'd see. I knew he was right. But leaving Jade … My inner-wolf was going crazy, clawing at my chest and pressing against my skin at the thought.

Another hand gripped my shoulder and tugged me around. "Look," Mark said. "Dammit, Aidan, look!"

And I did. I looked at my pack, bleeding and cut up. Some were limping; some could barely stand. Dominic was hunched over, his back torn up and bleeding. My pack was a mess, and I knew damn well if I forced them to attack now, we'd lose. We'd lose the war, and we'd put the girls in even more danger.

My pack needed me, but I couldn't just walk away. Not from her. Not from any of them.

I swallowed hard and jogged over to Dominic, dropping to my knees beside him. "You good?" I asked, which was probably a stupid question seeing as I'd been pretty certain that he was dead only a few minutes ago.

"Yeah," he said. "I'm good." He was still breathing roughly, but he looked better — steadier. More color in his cheeks. More of the typical coolness in his gaze. He looked more like Dominic and, well, less dead.

"Good." I reached out and clasped his shoulder. "I need you to do something for me."

Dominic nodded. It didn't look like an agreement, but more that he knew that now wasn't the time to disagree.

"Take them back to that hunting camp we passed about five miles out. Get them shifting. Get them healed as fast as you can."

Dominic looked sick, and he wouldn't look at me. "Don't," he said faintly and pulled back from me. "Don't ask me to leave her."

"I'm not asking, Dom," I said. "Go."

♥

There was a dull thump of flesh hitting the ground, and then another.

Beck and Mark were breathing hard beside me, and

low growls rumbled in their chest. I wasn't one hundred percent sure if those growls were a warning for me to stay hidden or if they were caused by what was happening just past the tree line from where we were crouched, watching in disbelief.

The cougars hadn't been taking the girls to the cabin. They'd been taking them to the cages.

My lips were curled back in a silent snarl, and I pawed at the ground restlessly, watching as, one by one, my females landed into the cages with a fleshy thump.

And still, the enforcers wouldn't let me attack.

Craig's teeth were pressing against my leg, holding onto the spot where the break had only just healed. The three of them had held back to help me, they said, but I knew the truth. They were here to make sure I didn't do anything stupid, and Craig's sharp teeth were a constant reminder of that.

Seventeen men were surrounding the cages, watching and laughing when the man who'd been talking to Jade at her window carried her over. She was relaxed into unconsciousness, her head resting lightly at his neck. He didn't drop her like the others. Instead, he set her down gently and brushed the hair from her face tenderly. It looked as if he actually cared about her. His hand lingered at her cheek for a moment that was way too long, and then he pulled a blanket around her.

My silent snarl turned into a loud growl. *I'm going to kill them all.*

I started forward, and Craig's teeth tightened onto my leg, pinching into my skin. I spun, snapping out at him. My heart was racing. *No one touched her like that. No one but me.* My inner-wolf wanted blood, and right then, all I could see was red.

Footsteps pounded in our direction and then slowed

as if the men couldn't figure out where the sound of my growl had come from. And Craig, damn him, he wasn't backing down. His teeth dug in deeper, and he started dragging me backward.

Beck launched at me then, growling and snarling, and Mark was right there with him. I let my scent roll off of me, growling at them to back down, but they didn't. My damn enforcers just kept coming, pushing and pulling me back, shuddering through the effort to ignore my commands. And it was then that I realized they were doing exactly what they were meant to do. Protecting my pack from me. Stopping me from making a move that could hurt them all.

And as they dragged me away before the cougars could find us, I didn't know whether I hated them or loved them for doing their damn job.

CHAPTER 23

JADE

I came awake feeling sick, achy, and cold. Someone was poking thick, blunt needles into my skin, or at least that's what it felt like, and when I tried to move, the world tilted and spun around me.

I blinked my eyes and groaned. It wasn't needles poking at me. It was wire. I was in one of those damned barbed wire cages.

I tilted my head slowly to the side and swallowed down the well of panic that bubbled up inside me when I realized that I wasn't alone. Curled up in the fetal position, Erika was pressing into the corner of the cage I was in. She was head to head with Laura, who was lying crookedly, bending with the other corner, and both were still out of it. And beside us in a second cage was Kristen, Stacy, Jo, and Whitney, all curled together in the center, unconscious.

I swallowed thickly and closed my eyes. How had it come down to this? My team, all six of them, were with me, split up and crammed into cages.

"You promised," I whispered, blinking away the sting of tears that bit at my eyelids. "You told me you wouldn't let me fail them." But Tommy wasn't here to hear me, and all I could do at that moment was hope that he'd gotten away. Maybe he'd found Aidan. Maybe he was safe. *Please let him be okay.*

Someone had draped a blanket over me, covering me up, and as I scanned over the girls, I noticed they had them, too. It was still daylight. The sun was high in the sky. I couldn't have been out long. No more than thirty minutes, I guessed. Everything felt foggy. I remembered the smiley face guy, and I remembered attacking him. The girls had started to shift. Tommy had been beside me, snarling. And then there was pain. Burning, hot pain.

"You shouldn't have brought them here," a deep, smooth voice said, and I blinked my eyes open again. It was smiley face guy, but he wasn't smiling, and for just a second, I thought that I saw something in him. Something other than the poison. He was looking at me with something that looked a lot like ... remorse?

"I shouldn't have brought who here?" I asked and sat up, swallowing down nausea that washed over me from the movement.

"Your mate, his males." He shook his head. "You shouldn't have brought them." His voice was very quiet, thoughtful, and almost sad. "We're going to have to kill them now."

My heart started racing. "I don't know what you're talking about." I almost shouted it, and I gritted my teeth, attempting to control my tone. "The only male I brought was in the truck with me. Where is he? Where's Tommy?"

He ignored my question and moved closer to the cage. He gave me an amused look and chuckled softly. "Yes, you do. You know exactly what I'm talking about." His right shoulder was covered in dried blood, and for a beat, I felt a bubble of delight, knowing that I'd caused at least a little damage before I'd been taken down. "We're going to find him," he said. He smiled then, a friendly, welcoming kind of smile that was more than a little confusing given the fact that he'd locked me up in a cage. "And we'll kill him when we do."

"Find who?" I asked, but I thought I already knew the answer to that. Even though it was terrifying to do that with him so close, I closed my eyes. I didn't want him to see what I felt, even if he could smell it. I didn't want to give him the satisfaction of seeing the way his words were ripping me in half.

Aidan left us here. He. Left. Us.

"Your mate," he said after a long moment. "It's too bad, though. We really could have used you both." He seemed so rational. Even his scent. It was calm. And it was ... my nostrils flared. I could smell cougars all around, but his scent, it was different. It was human.

My dad wasn't the only real shifter here.

I suddenly felt as though I'd been punched in the gut, and all my insides had been torn out. I felt hollow, empty.

And stupid. Really, really stupid.

Of course, Dad wouldn't leave his pack for days, or even weeks at a time without someone else here to keep them loyal. Things started to make sense. The fast changes in the cougars' location, even when Dad was home. He never seemed frazzled, always confident that he'd win his sickening games, and I guessed that was because he wasn't the only one playing them. He had someone else, someone like him who was after the same goal.

I opened my eyes. "You're like my dad, aren't you?" It came out as a half-whisper, half-shout. "You're not a werecougar. You smell like them, but it's not as strong. You're probably wearing clothes they'd worn, or maybe it's a transfer scent from being closed up with them in that small cabin. But you smell ..." I shook my head and pulled in another breath. "You smell more human right now than anything else. You've been calling the shots here while my dad was in Dog Mountain playing his games with my pack."

He didn't say anything, but his widening smile and soft chuckle were enough of a response for me to know that I was right.

"What's your name?" I asked, and my voice sounded all wrong. It was higher than normal, scratchy, too. My throat was dry, rough, and I swallowed — hard.

"It's Jason," he said and moved closer until he was right next to the cage. He rested his hands on top, bending his fingers loosely into the squared mesh, carefully avoiding the barbs, and looked straight down at me.

I fought back the urge to whimper and scuttled back. If Aidan and the team left me here, it was because they knew I could keep the girls safe, and I wasn't going to let this jerk think anything different, even if I was the one in a cage. "What happened to Tommy?" I demanded, and he raised his brows. "Where's the guy that came with me, Jason?"

Jason locked his gaze on mine and held it, losing his amused expression. "He's fine for now, and he'll stay fine if you cooperate."

I sucked in a breath. I bet it wasn't hard to miss the wave of misery that came from my scent because that was exactly how I felt — miserable. "I brought you what you asked for," I said and waved a hand toward the girls, but my voice totally lacked the conviction it needed to make the statement even semi-believable.

"It's not about the girls," he said. His voice started out soft but quickly hardened. "And we both know they were never meant to stay here. Your pack wouldn't have been hiding in the woods if they were."

He paused and stared down at me for an uncomfortable minute. "Jeff told you what he wants. What we want." He crouched down beside me, and his eyes flared with heat. Then he shrugged. "You should have thought of that before you tried to fool us with that stupid deal of yours."

Right, I thought, and then dread hit me. *He wants our packs to join together.*

"Where's my dad?" I asked. "I want to talk to him. Now."

"He's out hunting your mate." Jason sounded calm enough, but the tips of his ears were turning red, and the look in his eyes had gone completely insane.

I couldn't find any words. I just sat there shivering, staring into those crazy eyes. They were cold and calculating, searching my face like an invasive probe, and after a second, I found myself looking down.

"You can stop this," he said softly. "Order your males to join us. Make your females behave. If you work with me, I'll see what I can do about these cages."

I raised my head very slowly. "What?"

"Help me, and I'll let them out. This doesn't have to be ..." he paused and licked his lips, his hard eyes heating further. "Uncomfortable."

"Those bastards aren't going to find him, Jade," Erika said, and I jumped, twisting around to see her still curled in the fetal position. "Don't make a deal with this asshole." She glared at me. Her eyes were rimmed with red, but they were dry and really angry. "Don't you dare give up on Aidan or on us."

She stopped talking, and her eyes refocused on Jason, who stood up and was striding toward her. He watched her for a second, and she seemed to be holding her breath until he glanced back at me, and it whooshed out of her.

"Think about it, Jade," he said. "I'd be a good ally to have." And then he walked away.

By the time he vanished around the corner, my brain was working in overdrive. We had to get out of here before they found Aidan and the rest of the pack. There were no two ways about that. I looked at the cage, the chains, the barbs, the locks ...

An idea, not much of one, but it was something nonetheless, started to form. I looked back to Erika. "Wake up the girls," I said. "We've got to get out of here and help the others." I might have sounded calm and neutral, but right then, I was anything but. And I was pretty sure Erika knew that because she didn't waste a second in doing what I asked.

CHAPTER 24

AIDAN

Dominic stepped back from the door and closed it. He'd been hovering since I'd arrived. "They're close," he said. "A few more shifts, and we should be ready to move."

"How about you?" I asked, scanning his back. "Your back's still raw. You should be out there shifting with them."

"I should be with Jade." It wasn't the first time he'd said that since I'd gotten here and I hated hearing it. His tone held so much loathing, and his hatred was just boiling over. It wasn't making the call I'd made to send the pack away any easier to deal with.

I took a deliberate breath and then let it out, trying to keep my inner-wolf locked up tight. "You think it was easy leaving her there?" I asked. "You think I wanted to walk away? What was I supposed to do, Dom? Force you all to go in there when most of you could barely walk? How well do you think that would have played out?"

I felt sick leaving the girls. Utterly sick. Leaving them with those monsters was almost worse than seeing Dominic motionless on the ground. Almost.

The only thing that made it not as bad was that I knew, *I knew*, that Jeff wouldn't let them get hurt until he had what he wanted — my pack. And I wasn't going to give him that.

Beck, Mark, and Craig had dragged me, biting and clawing, pretty much the whole five miles to where my pack was holed up, trying to heal. They'd fought me hard every step of the way. Pushing through my scent, struggling against my commands. If I wasn't so pissed about it, I'd probably be amazed at how strong they were as a team. When one started to cave under my command, the others had picked up the slack, sensing each other's shortfalls and filling in the weaknesses. Yeah, okay, even if I was pissed off about it, it was still pretty amazing. They really were great together as a team.

But even if they were right, and we'd needed to regroup to be of any use to the girls, it felt ... sick leaving them and the kids there. Sick and wrong and cruel.

Right now, I had the pack outside shifting over and over. Deep cuts and bad breaks could take hours to heal, but shifting, well, it sped up the healing process, forcing the ripped-up skin and broken bones to reshape and mold and mend with each shift until they snapped back to how they were supposed to be.

My leg and all the new bites the enforcers had given me as they forced me back were as good as new after three shifts, but Dominic wouldn't do it. He was too damn focused on hating me to look after himself.

Dominic's hands curled into fists, and his face flushed an ugly red. "She's in a cage! They're all in a cage! You saw them put her in there, and you walked away."

A sudden surge of illness swept over me as the vision of Jade being carried and placed in that cage filled my head. She'd been out cold, and I'd watched as that guy that had stood at her truck window brush her hair back from her face with a tender sweep of his hand, and then he'd laid a blanket over her body.

It had taken everything in Beck, Mark, and Craig to stop me from charging in and trying to kill them all to get to her. There'd been seventeen cougars by the cages, watching my females being locked up. *Seventeen.* I hadn't spotted Tommy, but I had to assume that they'd have others watching him. There were thirty of us, including Jade, Tommy, and me. I didn't know where Tommy was exactly, and seven of my wolves were now in cages. If I was playing the numbers game, which I definitely was not doing anymore, I'd have to say our packs were close in numbers now. We'd killed another thirteen of them during their tree jumping stunt, but there were still at least those seventeen left.

And then I saw Dominic lying on the forest floor, not moving, and I remembered thinking he was dead, and I felt as if I were going to throw up.

"Yeah, Dom," I said, swallowing hard. "They're in cages, and that means that the cougars want to keep them alive. They're probably safer there right now than they would be with us." I scrubbed at my face, and when I looked back at him, Dominic started to speak, but I held up my hand to stop him. "I already thought I'd lost you once today. Couldn't go through that again, man. I just couldn't. They would have killed you if I'd let you go in after her. But they won't kill her. They need her to command our pack."

That threw him off for a second. His eyes went vague and unfocused. His hands started to uncurl, and his lips parted. "Is that ..."

"Dominic," I said, my voice deadly soft. "What I need right now is you backing me, not fighting me. That girl trapped in that damn cage means everything to me." I swallowed, and I pushed off the wall, turning away from him, mainly because my eyes had started to burn, and I seriously didn't want him to see it. "She's my home. I'm going to get her out of there."

There was silence for a long second before Dominic cleared his throat. "Um, is it safe to speak yet, or are you going to bite my head off?"

"What?" I asked, and all the breath left me in an audible huff with the word.

"Is that what you thought?" he asked hesitantly. "That I was dead?"

"Yeah," I said, and damn, I had to squeeze my eyes shut for a moment. I was fighting with all kinds of emotions — anger at Jade's dad, frustration with the entire situation, fury that my dad had pulled Chris home before I was ready, outright fear that I was going to lose someone close to me. So far, not one of my pack members had died today, and it scared the hell out of me that that could still happen.

"Shit, that must have sucked," he said and laughed a little, but there was no humor in the sound.

"Yep." I turned to him, and somehow I managed a small smile. "It did."

His blue eyes searched mine, and I knew he could see the emotion, but he didn't call me on it. "So," he said. "I'm going to go shift a few times, see if I can fix the gaping hole in my back. Five minutes and we should be good to go."

He started for the door, stopped, and grabbed me in a hug. I rocked back a little from the impact, but I hung on for a few beats, and with a couple of back slaps, we stepped apart.

"I thought you were dead," I said, and damn, my voice was all choked, but I found myself repeating it. "I thought you were dead."

"Yeah, we established that." Dominic gave me a

half-smile that looked kind of grim. "Come on," he said. "Let's go see if they're ready."

♥

I wasn't sure if the pack that stood before me was ready exactly, but they were determined, and I figured that had to count for something.

The sun was starting to fall on the horizon, and with only a couple hours of daylight left, we really needed to move. There was no way that I'd leave the girls there overnight, and by the looks set on my werewolves' faces, they weren't about to do that either.

There were twenty-two of us, all semi-dressed in a mix of camouflage and worn denim, that we'd found in the cabin. The air was cool with a breeze, and the forest around us was silent and still.

I thought I should say something epic and probably something motivating, but as I stared at them watching me, waiting, the only thing that came out of my mouth was, "I love her."

As it turned out, the pack thought those words were, in fact, epic. Cheers rose in the air, clapping and shouting, followed. I heard rumbles about alpha pairs and love and true partnership, and something about a new dawn for our pack. And for a brief moment, I was stunned silent.

"I can't promise you that we'll all walk away from this," I said, shouting over the cheers. I waited for a second for them to tamper down and continued. "And if you want to walk away, I won't blame you. You've all fought hard, and I'm grateful. But I can't ... I won't leave without our females and those kids. I won't go home without my mate." I paused for a moment and scanned the crowd, and then asked, "Are you with me?"

"Hell yeah," Beck shouted. "Wouldn't miss a good fight for anything."

But the rest of the pack was quiet, thoughtful. I was starting to get a little nervous that they would give up and go home, and then Phil walked up to me, and I had to admit that my nervousness tripled. He wasn't all for Jade being alpha, and he'd made that pretty clear in front of everyone when she'd walked into the headquarters with me after she'd moved out of her dad's house.

He stood in front of me for a moment, his eyes giving nothing away, and then he smiled. It wasn't really a happy smile, but it was an easy one. He extended his hand, and I took it in a shake. "I'm with you, kid, till the end."

More cheers, louder this time, and I smiled a real, full smile. They were with me. Even after all the bullshit Jade and I had made them suffer through, they were with me.

CHAPTER 25

JADE

The blankets were old and fraying, and they were really easy to tear.

The edges of the cages were wired together with more of the same sharp barbs that lined the walls. They weren't huge, at least not for three or four people, but they weren't small, either. The cage doors were chained closed with heavy locks securing them. Breaking those locks was a no-go. I'd tried. We'd all tried. We'd also tried to bend the barbed wire walls, pulling and tugging, but we couldn't break it. The damn thing just bent, and with the way the wire crisscrossed in small squares, even with bending the wire, we couldn't get an opening big enough to squeeze more than an arm through.

So now we were tearing up the blankets, wrapping our hands, and slowly untwisting the barbs that held the cages together along the edges. It was tedious and painful and frustrating as all hell, and I really didn't think a human would have the strength in their fingers to do it, but we did. And it was working. So far, we'd managed to loosen the top four inches on each cage door.

Erika hissed and jerked her hand back. "They couldn't have left us thicker blankets," she muttered under her breath, glaring at the corner of our cage and sucking on a finger. She huffed loudly. "We're never getting out of here." She sounded like she was fighting hard to sound normal, but she missed her mark. I could hear the panic building in her voice. I could smell it, too. And that bittersweet scent was choking me.

"Yes, we will," I said. I didn't sound normal, either. I sounded angry and hurt, and betrayed. I swallowed hard and attempted to ignore the sting that Aidan's leaving me here caused. He had his reasons. I knew that. If he thought he'd be able to get in and get us out safely, he would have. And I had no doubt he'd come back. He wouldn't just leave us here. But it still stung.

Keep it together! Be strong for them. I swallowed down the pain and whispered fiercely, "I'm going to get you all out of this." And I would, definitely, hopefully.

Erika shook her head. "Jade ..."

"I want cookies," Laura blurted suddenly and made a loud, frustrated sound from the back of her throat. "You'd think they'd at least give us comfort food after locking us up in these stupid cages."

I heard the shuffling footsteps coming behind me, and alarm shot through me. I scrambled, just like the others were, to pull my blanket up around me and hide the torn strips under it. Laura had taken up the job as our lookout, and since she loved to bake, she'd chosen *cookies* as the code for *someone was coming*, claiming that she'd be able to ramble on about them easily if anyone came by. She hadn't been lying. So far, she'd given out five recipes, talked about oven temperatures for baking them, and she'd even listed off her favorites and why.

"Really, Laura," Kristen said and rolled her eyes.

"Cookies again? Can't you find something else to go on about?"

Laura laughed as the man stalked by us, but it was a little strained. She shrugged. "What can I say? I love cookies."

He didn't come close to the cages. None of them had yet. Not since Jason had been here. This one looked a bit older than Jason but of a similar build and height. He didn't smile. He didn't frown. His expression was as flat as his muted brown eyes. Those eyes, though, stayed fixed on the girls right up until he rounded the corner and disappeared from sight.

At least they were leaving us alone. It was the best we could hope for, really, but it was also the one thing that knotted me up the most.

Because if they were leaving us alone, it meant that they were busy doing something else — like hunting my mate.

Once he'd turned the corner, Erika reached out for me, clutching onto me as if she thought that if she let go, she'd fall. Her head bent, and she rested it on my shoulder. She was shivering, and the shudders went right through me.

For a second, I was shocked because, well, it was Erika, and we weren't really on hugging terms, but the shock faded. I pulled her closer and held on just as tight. "It's going to be okay," I said. "I'm going to get you guys home."

She leaned back and looked at me. Her eyes were rimmed red, and she looked hollow and exhausted. "Jade, I-I'm so sorry."

I blinked in surprise. "You? Sorry?" I studied her for a second. "Sweetie, you've got nothing to be sorry for."

"Yes, I do," she said. "I'm sorry for ignoring your calls and for messing around with Aidan and for being a crappy beta." She wiggled away from me and grabbed the edge of a blanket, tearing off another strip. "I shouldn't have let him in that day. I should have answered the phone. I shouldn't have told you I was studying. I was just ..."

"Erika, stop," I said, taking her trembling hand and squeezing it. "Just stop. It's over. We're good, okay? None of that matters anymore." I meant it, and by the look she gave me, I knew she was aware that I was serious. Whatever happened before was over, done, buried. The whole thing seemed kind of ridiculous now, given our situation.

I squeezed her hand one more time, and then I snagged up one of the strips of fabric and quickly wrapped up my fingers before shifting back over to the corner I'd been working on and starting in on the next barb.

She was silent for a moment, and then almost awkwardly, she said, "When Aidan showed up at my door, he looked so wrecked, and you ... you were being so stupid. God, Jade, you walked away from him. He's the best thing that's ever happened to you. We all saw it. The way you looked at him like he was *it* for you, and he saw you, too. It was like no one else existed for him except you, and you just walked away. I was so mad at you for that. I would have killed to have what you two have." She laughed then, a strangled kind of laugh. "Turns out I did. I just didn't realize it until it was too late."

I looked at Erika, really looked at her, and I saw something. Something in her teary eyes made me feel a little helpless. And guilty. Crazy guilty. The truth was that I kind of hated me, too, for walking away. If I had have stuck it out, forgiven Aidan sooner, and worked with him to stop my dad, instead of unknowingly helping Jared inflict his revenge, we probably wouldn't have been stuck in a cage.

I didn't even know what to say.

But I did know who she was referring to. Craig. I knew she was really hung up on him, and I thought the other women knew that, too. They were all looking at her with that *you poor thing* look, and all I wanted to do was fix it for her. It was ... weird and really unexpected, but she was mine. My female, my wolf, part of my pack, and it tore me up seeing her so ... sad.

"It's kind of scary, isn't it?" I said. "Loving someone that much." I shook my head. "I wasted so much time with Jared, you know? Time that I could have had with Aidan. At first, I told myself it was because I wanted to stop my dad, and Jared was the way to do that, but really it was because I was scared. Terrified, actually. Aidan lied to me, manipulated me into fighting for him, for the pack, and for you guys." I laughed once. "Turns out it was probably the best thing he'd ever done."

"Yeah," she breathed. "It's freakin' terrifying."

I looked back at the corner and started twisting the wire again. "If you want my advice, don't stop fighting, Erika. Never stop fighting. Life is too short not to spend it with the person who makes you whole."

"She's right," Jo said. "If he's important, you need to fight for him. But if you ask me, Craig's the one screwing this up. Not you. The way I heard it, he hadn't even told you that he wanted you as his mate until after the Aidan thing."

"We were sort of seeing each other," Erika said. "It was casual, but it was still something."

Kristen snorted. "Casual. All that means is that he's too chicken to make a commitment. When you get that boy back, you make sure he knows you aren't playing around this time."

"Did you bring me cookies this time?" Laura

shouted, and we all jumped and shuffled, hiding our escape efforts as fast as we could.

It was a long, long afternoon. Eventually, the men stopped walking by. I wasn't really sure if that was a good thing or not, but without their constant observation, we made headway on our exit strategy. Another ten minutes or so, and we'd be able to shove the doors open. We didn't talk much, just worked. There didn't seem to be a lot to talk about after the girls had determined that it was Craig that was being an idiot. I wasn't entirely sure if I completely agreed with that. She'd hurt him. Crushed him, actually. But it made Erika a little less teary-eyed to hear it, so it was good.

The sun was starting to fall when I heard the bell-like laughter. It was sweet, almost like wind chimes, and it was followed by a full-bellied, rumbling laugh that I'd have known anywhere.

I froze mid-twist and whispered, "Shush. My dad's here." I didn't know what else to say, but the round of fast, suction-like breaths made me very aware that the girls knew that him being here probably wasn't a good thing.

Because if he was here, then the chances were good that he'd found my pack, and Aidan wasn't coming back for us.

Dad had his arm around a tiny young girl with a head of blond, ringlet curls. She couldn't have been more than twelve. He was smiling down at her as he strode toward us. It was the smile he'd always given me. The one that said I was the absolute center of his world. The one that made me feel warm and loved, and safe. And seeing it directed at someone else stung — bad. So bad that my chest ached and my eyes burned.

Behind him were a bunch of his cougars, eight, no, there were nine of them. They looked happy and really excited. And it made my inner-wolf, and me, hurt, a deep, sharp ache that filled every part of my body.

I tried (and failed) to bury the feeling as I lifted my chin and gave Whitney a narrowed smile. She quickly slid back, covering the corner of the cage they'd been working on, and at the same time, Laura took up the position in our cage.

Dad stopped and crouched down in front of the girl. "Go see what your brothers are getting into, pumpkin," he said. "I'll be in soon, okay?"

She smiled, a radiant, sunshine kind of smile, and giggled. "Will you play that card game with me?" Her voice was just like her laugh, sweet and bell-like.

"Sure," he said. "Now, go on." And with a quick kiss on his cheek, she turned and ran back around the corner, and a second later, I heard the door to the cabin open and then slam shut.

"Did I miss a chapter?" Erika whispered. "Because that looked like a man who loves that little girl."

"Yeah, it did," I said quietly, not wanting him to overhear. I felt sick. Cold and sick and hurt. "That was exactly how he was with me until I met Aidan." And I couldn't help but wonder if that girl was meant to be more than a girl who wound up in a cage because I was sure there had to be something more to that kindness, just like there had been when he used it with me. For me, he'd used it to steer me closer to Dominic and the pack, and I was sure he was using it on her to point her in whatever direction he needed her to go in. His pushes for me had always been subtle and always hidden behind that *I love you* smile, but when I thought about it, really thought about it, they'd been there. Always. For years now.

Dad asked where Jason was, and I didn't think he liked the answer because his eyes hit mine then, and they were bright with anger. He closed the distance to the cage with a long, determined stride and pointed at me. "Stand up, move to the door, and don't you give me any lip, Jade. I'm not going to tolerate it."

I didn't stand up. Instead, I only blinked, stunned by the harshness in his voice. Was he completely done pretending to care about me? Had he ever actually cared? There wasn't a trace, not even a tiny speck of warmth in his eyes as he glared at me. Nothing. It was as if I meant nothing to him anymore, and I found myself crouching, getting ready to shift if I had to. The girls were silent, stiff, and ready, too.

"You should have listened to me, Dad," I said. "You should have run."

He gave me a long, frowning look. "Stand up, Jade. It's time we come to some kind of agreement here."

"I'm not leaving my girls in here," I shot back with a touch of a growl, deepening my tone. "You want to talk to me, talk because I'm not going anywhere without them."

His eyes narrowed. "I'm not giving you a choice. I've played your little game long enough."

"My game!" I shouted. There was something in his tone that made my spine snap straight, and my entire body tensed up tight. "I was never playing a damn game."

"Watch that tone with me, Jade," Dad growled. "I'm still your father even if you choose to pretend I'm not."

I crossed my arms, holding the blanket snuggly in place. "It's a little late for fatherly lectures, Dad. You lost that right the moment you threw me out of the house and pushed me into becoming Aidan's mate."

Dad lowered his voice, and his eyes were suddenly intense. "I did that for you." He sounded like he actually meant that. "None of this would be possible if you weren't mated to him. I've given you power. I've given you the backbone you needed to run your pack and mine."

"Why the hell would I want to run a pack of sick male cougars who think it's okay to lock women in cages and use them as toys?" I glanced past him to the men who'd gathered behind him and snarled. "What's wrong with you people?"

At one time, I'd wondered if maybe they weren't all evil. I'd hoped for it, actually. But as I looked at them, they didn't even have the decency to look ashamed. A few of them even chuckled. These weren't good but misguided people. They were monsters. All of them.

"Everyone has their vices, pumpkin." Dad had the courtesy to look away, but I really wondered if it was only because his left eye had started to twitch, and he didn't want me to see it.

I shook my head. "This isn't a vice. In the real world, it's called kidnapping, rape, and murder."

"We're shifters, pumpkin." His voice softened, and he moved, rounding the cage to the doorway. He still wasn't looking directly at me, only watching me from the corner of his eye. "The rules are different for us."

He sounded as if he actually believed the garbage he was spewing at me. Like this was normal behavior, accepted even. How scary was that? The man who raised me, loved me, cared for me, actually thought that what he was doing, what he allowed his pack to do, was okay.

"Do you actually hear yourself?" I asked. I aimed for disgust, except my voice came out as a whisper. "Shifter or not, this isn't okay, Dad."

"I'm done discussing this with you," he snapped. His face grew red and furious as he reached into his pants pocket and fished out a key. "If you want to see Aidan again, you'll stand up and come over to the door."

Panic, blind, hot panic set in as he leaned forward to

unlock my door. We'd left the wires on, but loose, to keep the doors looking solid as the men walked by, but if he grabbed it, the top half would flutter and give.

"He's not here," I said, scrambling forward and blocking the girls in my cage behind me and out of his reach. "I'd scent him if he was." I was glad I sounded confident in that because I didn't feel it. My heart was hammering so hard that it hurt to breathe.

"Well," Dad said, taking hold of the lock, "you can believe that if you want to, pumpkin, but he's here. My boys found him, and they're here for their reward. You can come with me and see him, or you can stay here and watch."

The door started to bend as he fiddled with the key, and his eyes, blazing with fury, snapped to mine. He opened his mouth, probably to yell at me, but didn't get a chance. "No!" Whitney shouted. "No, don't touch me!" And the wire door on the second cage clambered to the ground.

"Look at this," one of the men said. The disbelief was obvious in his voice. "These girls were fixing to escape."

And then everything seemed to blur together. There was laughter, cold, cruel laughter, bones breaking, and growls sounding. The men crowded the cage; the girls shifted.

Dad tore off the door to my cage, and he dropped to his knees. He glared at me long and hard, and then he pressed forward. His arm leaped out, and he wrapped his hand around my ankle, pulling hard.

"Back up," I growled, kicking out of his hold. "Don't make me hurt you."

But he didn't back up. He only laughed. And it was then that I decided that he was dead to me. Completely and officially dead to me.

CHAPTER 26

It was a calm, easy trek back to the werecougars' location, though I had to admit, I was waiting for something to go wrong. As we reached the edge of the forest where the cougars had hidden in the trees, I thought that we'd face another attack.

But nothing happened.

The only thing we found waiting for us were the dead we'd left behind. The cougars hadn't even bothered to collect their pack members. I almost felt bad for the dead — almost.

Most of the space around the cages was taken up by the werecougars. Some were shaking the structures, taunting the girls trapped inside. They'd shifted to wolves, and were growling, a low, deadly threat that didn't seem to faze the werecougars. A few of the men stood by and watched, but all of them looked ... hungry, greedy, eager.

Jeff himself was on his knees, half in and half out of the cage Jade was in. He had a hand on her ankle, and he was pulling as if he thought he could physically drag her from the confines of the barbed wire enclosure.

He wasn't getting far.

Jade looked stubborn, but there was something else there, too. Despair. I could smell it. She was putting up a good fight, but she struggled to keep it together. She kicked wildly at her father as he pulled at her legs, but she wasn't making any of the kicks count. And she was yelling, except I had no idea what she was saying. It was garbled and frantic, a string of sounds that didn't quite sound like words. She had Erika, and I was pretty sure Laura, trapped behind her. They were snapping out at Jeff, though, they couldn't quite reach around Jade to hit their intended mark.

I growled. I could almost feel her fear, and I wanted, no, I needed her to calm down and focus. I channeled my alpha scent, letting it pour out of me. There was a good breeze flowing through the forest, and I figured it would only take a few seconds for her to pick up my scent, and I seriously hoped smelling me close by would be enough to make her chill out.

It worked.

Suddenly, Jade just stopped. She stopped yelling. She stopped struggling. She looked toward me, her eyes squinting as she scanned the trees, and she laughed a little hysterically.

The other females were snarling, snapping, growling, within the other cage, but as Jade laughed, they stopped, too, sitting back on their hind legs, panting.

They knew we were here.

As evidence to that, Jade laughed again, looked straight at her father, and said loudly, "You better let go of me now." She sounded a little sad but also really furious. "Aidan's not really a fan of people trying to hurt what's his, and neither is my pack. When they find out what you were planning to do, they'll kill you all."

For a beat, there was nothing but silence. The men paused in their taunting. They turned, following the females' gazes, but they didn't move.

And then I noticed that it wasn't just Jade's cage that was open. The doors, both of them, were completely off and lying on the ground. Maybe that was the reason they hadn't moved; nothing would be blocking the exit for my females if they did.

"Ignore her," Jeff growled. "Man up and get those wolves under control." He started pulling at Jade again, but when she kicked, she hit him square in the face. He sat back, and his hand shot up to his nose, and he shouted, "You little brat!"

I felt a dark, bloodthirsty thrill spread through my belly, and I let the rush of adrenaline wash over me. I started to shift. It was probably crazy taking my human form now, but I wanted Jeff to know it was me. I didn't want there to be any doubt in his mind that the wolf who ended his sick, miserable life was me. And my inner-wolf, well, it seemed he wanted that, too. He didn't put up a fight; instead, he pushed the shift along, giving up all his control.

A soft tingle spread along my skin as the coarse black fur that covered my body began to recede. The snapping of my bones sounded extra loud, bouncing through the silent forest, but all I felt was the rush of the shift.

When my human body solidified, I got up to my feet and rolled my shoulders. I let out a slow breath, surveying the group. There were only nine of them, plus Jeff, by the cages, but I figured the others would come running the moment we attacked. Actually, I was counting on it.

Dominic growled and made a chomping sound with his teeth. He looked up at me and gave me a lopsided dog smile. He was ready to go. I just smiled back, although it probably looked a little feral. "Find the kids," I said. "Keep them away from the cages." And then, keeping my human form, I strode forward.

The werecougars seemed confused. Maybe they thought I was crazy, walking out into their midst; I wasn't sure. But then they looked past me, and alarm replaced the confusion. One of them made a startled sound, and they started to move, drawing back and flinching as my pack followed me, moving in from every direction. We moved in calmly. None of my wolves threatened. No one attacked. They were just there, a quiet, deadly presence at my back.

"You won't be keeping them, Jeff," I said with a lazy smirk, stopping a few feet from his back. "Step away from them before something ... unfortunate happens."

He didn't seem to care one way or another that I was standing there, which was odd, I thought, and definitely stupid. He barely even looked at me, keeping most of his focus on Jade.

But Jade was looking at me. Her eyes raked down my body, and a flush shaded her cheeks. "Hey, baby," she said and laughed a little. She sounded pretty close to insane, breakable, and stressed. Really, really stressed. She gave me a look that was half warm and half cold and crossed her arms, ignoring her father completely. "Took you long enough."

I grinned and shook my head. "Sorry, sweetheart. Won't happen again."

"You're darn right it won't." Her nose scrunched up, and she waved a hand widely around her. "Can you believe these guys actually think keeping me in a cage will convince me to force our wolves to join them?" She huffed. "And guess what else? Our females are supposed to be their reward for hunting you guys down. Dad here even said you were here, and he was going to let me see you if I let his beasts have our girls."

I chuckled. "Is that so?" *She was good at this*, I thought. Good at acting as if everything was normal, and she had the situation under control when she was really coming close to full-out panic. I could smell it. I could hear it in her laugh and see it in her eyes.

"Yep," she said and grinned. "But you don't look like you've been hunted down and caught, so I'm thinking he's full of crap."

A couple of my wolves pressed in closer to the cage beside Jade's, forcing the werecougars back with a few low growls, and as they moved further away from the cage, the females sprang free and quickly melted in with the rest of the pack.

"Sweetheart," I said gently. "You can go on and shift now. I've got this."

"Aidan," Jeff said, and finally leaned fully out of the cage and looked at me. He sounded annoyed, as if the last threads of his patience were thin and about to snap. "Don't encourage her. She's not leaving this camp. None of you are."

"Step away from my mate, Jeff," I said and took another step toward him. I gave him a second, only a second, to obey, and then I lunged forward, grabbed his ankles, and yanked him away from Jade.

He shouted, just a small, quick burst of sound. He kicked out at me, but it was too late. I already had him flipped onto his back and pinned to the ground.

The realization that I wasn't just here for my females must have dawned on him as my bones began to break and change. He looked up at me wide-eyed and pretty obviously scared. His fear smelled bittersweet. He tried to slide out from underneath me, but his panic made him slow, sloppy, and completely uncoordinated.

"What are you idiots waiting for?" he shouted. "Get this beast off me!"

CHAPTER 27

JADE

I couldn't shift.

It wasn't that I didn't want to, because I did. I really did. And my inner-wolf, well, she wanted out, and she wasn't being quiet about it either. My skin was crawling, and raw adrenaline was pumping through my body, but I just couldn't do it.

There was chaos all around me. Wolves and cougars. Snarling and hissing. My pack was taking them down faster than my brain could process. None of the cougars were running to help my dad. Okay, that wasn't entirely true. They were trying to get to him, but my wolves were taking them down before reaching their target.

Beck, a large dusty-gray wolf, stood at the cage door. He was whimpering and nudging at the bottom side of my foot, urging me to come out.

But I couldn't make myself move.

Those monsters were going to take my girls, and I hadn't been able to do anything to stop them.

Suddenly Aidan let out a war cry and threw a hard elbow right into my dad's jaw, and then he shifted. It all happened so quickly I almost missed the change.

His body hazed, bones broke, bent, changed, midnight black fur replaced tanned skin. He was snarling, growling, and pinning my dad down.

I watched it all, and I felt nothing.

This was it. My mate was going to kill my father, and I felt nothing.

Absolutely nothing.

I expected to feel something. Sadness or relief or anger. Something. Anything. But all I felt was numb.

Was it wrong that most of me wanted him to die? He was a monster. He'd kidnapped, raped, and killed, or he at least organized those horrible things, and his victims were innocent people — humans that had no chance of defending themselves against his pack. He deserved death. They all did.

Erika and Laura were nudging at me, trying to push me out of their way without hurting me. They wanted out. They wanted to help our pack, but I was frozen, caught up within my numbness, and blocking their exit.

Aidan's jaw was opened wide, and he was lowering, ready to rip out my dad's throat, but suddenly he made a painful sound, somewhere in the middle of a snarl and a whimper, and stumbled backward, rolling off my father.

Dad scrambled to his feet. He was holding a sharp-looking pocketknife in his hand that was stained and dripping scarlet liquid from its blade. He was bloody, too, and he looked weakened, but he was moving, and the sight sent my inner-wolf into a rage-endured frenzy within my chest. That man — my father — had been about to offer my wolves to his pack of beasts as a reward. He didn't deserve to be moving.

And that's when I felt something. Something dark and a little crazed, and it compounded into something that was totally insane.

I scrambled from the cage, the barbs tearing at my knees and catching at the blanket that was tucked snugly around me, almost ripping from my body.

My eyes were locked on the knife clasped in my dad's hand. "Who the hell brings a knife to a shifter fight?"

Dad didn't answer, but then I guess I didn't expect him to. He wasn't paying any attention to me, and he didn't seem to notice Erika and Laura, either. The girls were pressed to my side, snarling at him, as I advanced.

"Stand up to them!" he cried. He looked around, frantically waving the knife. "Make them submit."

The cougars were shifting, and more were coming. Running across the small yard, tearing off their clothes. The sound of bones snapping, so many at once, was a sickening sound, echoing back from the cabin and the forest walls.

"You're destroying everything, Aidan," Dad shouted, turning as Aidan got back to his feet and stalked toward him. He held his hands out, still clasping the small knife in one, as though his hands could stop my mate from coming closer. "Your emotions are clouding your judgment and stopping you from doing your job. You're supposed to be leading them, not fighting for a girl. Alpha pairs aren't about love. Strength and dominance are all that matters." His voice was rising, tinted with fear. "You said that yourself not so long ago in my living room. Be the dominant male you're meant to be and control your mate! Stop fighting me for a girl!"

Aidan's lips curled, and he let out a vicious snarl. I couldn't see his wound through his thick black fur, but I knew it was there. I could smell it, his pain and his blood, but he didn't let it show. He stalked toward my dad, and that was when my dad stumbled back, crashing into the cage that had held me captive. He dropped his knife, and it clattered through the wire, just as the cage bent, and then collapsed under his weight. He let out an agonized cry as the barbed wire tore through his clothing and ripped into his skin.

"No, Dad," I said. "You're wrong." I quickly rushed to Aidan's side, pressing my leg against his fur. He glanced at me, just a quick look, before letting out another growl at my father. "His emotions aren't clouding his judgment. They're making him see what's important. Leading a pack isn't all about power and control."

Dad tried to stand up, but he couldn't. Erika and Laura snarled and snapped each time he moved, pushing him back down. Dots of blood began to well up from where the barbs had dug into his skin. The more he struggled, the worse it got.

"You asked me about the women," he said. "This is why they aren't changed. This is why they don't live with us. He's going to lose everything because of you. Because he thinks he loves you."

I almost corrected him. Almost. But I didn't. It wasn't worth the breath to tell him that Aidan didn't *think* he loved me. He knew he did, just like I knew with him. I almost asked him about Mom, too, but again, I thought I probably didn't want to know. I didn't want to know if he actually cared about her or why he'd married her. I was sure the answer would only make me sick.

Instead, I looked over my shoulder and said softly, "Look around, Dad. We aren't exactly losing anything."

And we weren't. In minutes, my pack had taken down over half of Dad's forces, and they were still attacking with vehemence fervor.

That was when a cougar broke through my wolves and charged at us. He hit Laura first with a hard knock into her side that threw her to the ground. Erika spun away from my dad, baring her teeth, but she hesitated.

We all hesitated.

Because it wasn't a werecougar. It was a shifter. It was Jason. In mid-leap, he shifted into a bird, a big ugly looking bird. He flew upward and disappeared into the forest.

His little stunt gave Dad an opening. Dad launched from the cage and rushed at Aidan. He started to shift, and it cost him his life. Aidan might think twice about killing someone in human form, all of us would, but once the shift started, it was over.

I thought Dad knew that, too. He glanced at me, just a quick look that was cold and emotionless, and it told me he didn't regret anything he'd done, and then he was taken down.

Beck and Erika, who'd been circling around us, lunged forward to attack, and they latched onto his calves, causing him to fall. And then more wolves descended, biting into him and tearing at his flesh.

He started to scream, but it sounded all wrong. His voice wasn't human. It was rough and pitched and screechy. His face wasn't his anymore; it was something else, something not quite human and not fully animal, as though it had frozen in mid-shift, and I wasn't entirely sure what he'd intended to turn into.

I clamped my hand to my mouth, holding in my own scream. I wanted to look away, but I couldn't. It was as if I needed to see this, even if I didn't want to. I needed to know the terror he'd caused was over. I heard his last breath, and I saw his struggle stop. It was fast, and it was deadly, and it was a horrible way to die, being torn apart.

CHAPTER 28

AIDAN

It would have been better if Jade hadn't watched.

Jade wouldn't look away, even after her father took his last breath. Her eyes were wide and filled with horror. It was as if she were frozen, not wanting to watch and not able to move. I could hear her heart pounding within her chest, and her scent was thick and bitter.

A sickening crack filled the air, and she flinched, but still, she didn't look away.

I trotted over to her side and rubbed up against her leg, nudging her and nipping at the torn wool blanket that was wrapped snugly under her arms.

Her hand fell to my head, and that's when she finally tore her eyes away from her dad. They hit mine, and the horror faded into something that looked like worry. But she smiled a little. "I'm fine, Aidan," she said, and her body trembled through a shudder. She gave my head an absent little pat. "Go help the others." And then she turned and started to walk away.

I opened my mouth and let out a loud growl, protesting. She didn't look fine. She looked lost and kind of defeated, and if she looked around, she'd see that the pack didn't really need my help. The cougars were falling quickly, and the last few still fighting were battling against the team. Some of our pack had even started shifting back to human. The fight was pretty much over.

She stopped short at the sound of my growl and spun back to face me. "Don't growl at me," she said, placing a hand on her hip. She smiled tightly, the strain showing clearly in her features. "Go on. Find Tommy. I need to go and meet the kids."

I growled again, but it was useless. Her face was set in that stubborn determination. I knew that face, and I knew it well. No matter what I did or said, she would do what she thought she needed to do.

But still, I shifted anyway.

My inner-wolf didn't even try to stop me. I thought he was probably just as worried about her as I was.

With her hand still on her hip, Jade noticed and waited for me to get to my feet. I figured she knew I'd only chase after her if she started to walk away again. And as she waited, those big brown eyes of hers never left mine.

I stepped in close and pulled her into my arms. She didn't protest, not even a little. As soon as I touched her, her hand fell from her hip, and she wrapped her arms around my waist, holding onto me tightly.

"I wish you didn't watch that," I said, pressing my nose to her hair and breathing in a deep drag of her scent. "I'm sorry you did."

"I needed to see it." Her voice was freakishly composed, and she pressed her hand to my chest, pushing gently until I let her go. "Please find Tommy," she said. "I really want to go make sure those kids are okay."

I studied her for a moment and then nodded. "Sure,

sweetheart." And even though the last thing I wanted was to let her go, I stayed put and watched her walk away, although the entire time, I thought I should probably follow her. Actually, it was a serious effort not to follow her.

But I didn't, because well, I believed her. She really was okay.

My girl is okay.

When she rounded the corner of the cabin, I turned back to the yard, surveying the scene. Mark and Craig were finishing off the last werecougar standing. They were doing it quickly, efficiently, and with two well-placed bites, the beast laid limp on the ground.

And it was over.

All those weeks of games with Jeff, and it was finally over. It felt ... good. I felt ... lighter, knowing we'd stopped those monsters before they could hurt anyone else.

Beck had shifted, and he was jogging the tree line, with Landon on his heels. They were counting the dead, I realized, watching their lips move with the silent numbers. Beck noticed me and veered my way. "We got the thirteen from the tree jumping ambush and another sixteen down here," he said when he reached me. "But it looks like that other full shifter got away."

"What about our pack?" I asked. "Is everyone okay?"

"A few cuts, but nothing that won't heal," Landon said. "We found Tommy. He got snagged up in one of those tree snares. Everyone's accounted for."

I nodded and swallowed a few quick swallows. "Let's get the dead buried then," I said. Tension that I hadn't even realized was there melted from my shoulders and the knots in my gut loosened. "And then we go home. We've got some ashes to spread tonight."

Beck smiled. "Sure thing, boss," he said, and as they

took off, I turned back to the cabin and went to meet the kids.

JADE

Dominic and Luken were playing Go Fish, and they were losing.

I found the kids inside the cabin with Dominic and Luken. It wasn't much. One large room with bunk beds lining the back wall and what looked like a sleeping loft with a log-style ladder leading up. A propane stove, a small sink, and a large wooden fold-up table surrounded by chairs.

Dominic grumbled something under his breath as the girl with the blond ringlet curls snatched a card from his hand. He'd dressed — kind of — in an orange jacket that was open and far too small and a pair of camouflage pants, which were identical to Luken's get-up. The girl giggled, a delighted little giggle, and her cheeks were stained with an excited blush.

Not really what I'd expected to find, that was for sure.

A little boy, maybe three, tiptoed up beside Dominic and rose up on his toes. He had curly red hair, and his chubby little cheeks were dotted with freckles. He held a hand over his mouth, trying to hold in his giggles as he peeked at Dominic's cards.

He took a good look, and then, he ran over to the girl and whispered loudly, in a way only a child could. "He's got a two of hearts."

I laughed. I couldn't help it. As the one boy whispered, not so quietly, another boy about the same age was doing the tiptoe thing to Luken. He was adorable, with white-blond hair and crisp blue eyes, and he had a heart-stopping smile, with two little dimples.

Luken shifted in his chair, ever so slightly, and passed his cards from one hand to another, so the boy could get a better look without being too obvious about it.

I laughed again, harder this time, and Dominic looked up at me, grinning widely. "Tara's kicking my butt at cards," he said. "And Joel and Cody are helping her do it. They're all little cheats!"

"Is that Jade?" Tara asked. She looked up at me, and her pretty little smile vanished.

"That's her," Dominic said. He put his cards down and leaned back in the rickety-looking wooden chair.

She fixed me with a cool stare and folded her arms over her chest. "He said that you're going to make us go to school. He said we're going to live with your pack now. Is that true?"

"Do you want it to be true?" I asked hesitantly because I really couldn't tell if she liked the idea or not. Her scent said she was excited, but the body language ... well, it was cold and a little angry.

"Will my dads be coming with us?" she asked, her sweet-sounding voice turning harsh.

"Um ..." I started and then just stopped. I didn't know how to answer that. I wasn't sure if I should tell her the truth or sugarcoat it. I thought she probably heard the commotion outside, and I figured she was old enough to know what had happened. But still ... she was just a kid.

I looked to Dominic for some help, but he only shrugged as if to say he had no idea how to proceed.

As it turned out, I didn't have to say anything.

Suddenly, Aidan's warm weight settled in at my back, and his solid arm looped around my waist. "No, sweetheart," he said, "they won't be coming with us."

His tone was gentle, soft even. "Your dads had to go away."

She snorted and rolled her eyes. "You mean they're dead."

Somehow I hadn't quite expected the snark in her response or her blunt statement. I thought she'd be upset, maybe even shed some tears. I'd seen the way she'd been with my dad. I'd noticed the smile and the eager expression. And yes, I'd really thought it had been real.

But I was beginning to think that maybe she'd been playing the *sweet and innocent* card because the bottomless look in her eyes right then told me that she'd seen more horror in her short life than anyone should have seen.

I wasn't the only one that was left speechless by her statement. Dominic's eyes widened, and he sucked in a quick, sharp breath. Luken's jaw dropped, stunned.

I saw Erika, Laura, and Jo inch forward from the corner of my eye. They'd come in, probably behind Aidan, and I hadn't even noticed. I glanced over my shoulder quickly to find all of the females from my pack squashed in behind Aidan and me, and outside there were quite a few of the males hovering.

I felt equally shocked and proud at that moment, seeing my pack crowding into and around the cabin, making sure the kids were okay, that we were all okay, and it sent tingles all over my body.

If Tara had noticed them, she wasn't letting on. She kept her eyes fixed on Aidan, waiting for an answer.

He hesitated for a second, and then he sighed. "Yes, they're dead. They hurt a lot of people, sweetheart, and they weren't going to stop."

"I know." She looked down at her cards and frowned. "I saw Jade and her friends in the cages. I know what happens to the girls that go in there. My mom died in one of them a few months ago." She lifted her tiny shoulders in a shrug. "Too bad you didn't come sooner."

And right then, my heart broke. Just shattered.

There was a round of gasps from the pack, and the scent of their heartbreak spiked in the air. *I'm sorry* was murmured over and over, and I heard a few sobs, too.

"Sweetheart ..." Aidan said. His voice cracked, and his arm loosened from my waist. He started to step around me to go to her, and I noticed he'd fastened one of the blankets from the cages around his waist, covering him up.

But Tara didn't seem to want his sympathy. She held up a hand, asking him silently to stop, and said, "I like the idea of going to school. Dominic said there would be other girls my age there. Can I have my own bedroom when we move from here?"

"You can have anything you want, baby," I said, and there were tears in my voice. "Anything."

She nodded and watched me wearily for a moment before turning to her brothers. "Come on, boys," she said, standing up. "The faster you pack your things, the faster you'll get to play with that fire truck Dominic told you about."

They didn't waste any time jumping into action. As I watched them rush around packing up their belongings, I realized that not only had we killed my father and defeated the werecougars, but thanks to my incredible pack, we were going to give these three children a chance at real life.

After all the pain and misery, things were finally starting to look up, and I thought that today just might have been one of the worst, and probably the best, day of my life.

EPILOGUE

JADE

Aidan had promised that we'd do something boring when the battle with my dad was over. I couldn't say that boring was what I got, but I did get normal, and normal, well, that was just as good as boring.

The hallways in the pack headquarters were abnormally quiet for a Saturday. Everyone was tiptoeing around and whispering, and that could only mean one thing: the boys were having a nap.

I glanced back over my shoulder, taking one last peek at Tara as she strutted out of my temporary bedroom in her new knit dress. Dominic let out a whistle of approval, and I smiled, and then, I snuck away down the hall to track down Aidan and the two sleeping monsters.

It had been just over a week since we'd brought the kids home, and it had been nothing short of chaotic. We'd held Jared's service right after we got back from the hunting camp, spreading his ashes in the clearing. I'd been right; it had been a good thing for the team and for the pack. A little closure after a lot of death. And thanks to Marcy, it all went smoothly.

Mom had taken the kids during the service, and

well, I was pretty sure she fell in love with them during those two short hours. The kids, all three of them, were now living with her. She'd been adamant about it, and although both Aidan and I were planning on taking them in, we were also glad she'd said no to that idea, because well, we might be the alpha pair, but we were just barely adults ourselves, and definitely not ready to look after three children on a full-time basis. But being a big sister and brother was a heck of a lot of fun.

After the kids' living arrangements were settled, there were shopping trips and school registrations to handle. At first, those two things hadn't seemed like a lot, but it was. The kids had never been to a store. They'd literally lived their lives in the bush.

On the first trip to a mall, I thought I would have to rush Tara to the hospital. She'd hyperventilated herself into unconsciousness, passing out in the first store we went to that sold girls' clothing. Who would have thought buying a dress could be that epic? Well, for Tara, it was. She even told me so, over and over and over, and well, over again.

And the boys ... Aidan had taken them to a toy store, and let's just say that nothing — absolutely nothing — could have prepared him for that one.

During that experience, I decided that my mom wasn't just awesome; she was a superstar. Aidan had called her, explained the nightmare he'd found himself in, and she'd come to the rescue and quickly wrangled the boys.

On top of getting the kids settled in, Aidan and I had been living at the pack headquarters because our house was currently undertaking a massive overhaul. The carpets were being torn out, the walls repainted. Even the kitchen and bedrooms were being renovated.

And today was the day we'd finally get to move back in. I had to admit, I was crazy excited about that.

But even if it was hectic, it was normal, it was fun, and having the kids around, even if they weren't living with us, made everything a little ... better, easier. The kids were going to be okay, which made what we did, what the pack did, to stop my father, worth it.

As for the pack, well, life just went on. Some went back to work, others went back to school. Things just went back to normal. Okay, maybe not entirely normal; we were werewolves after all, but it was all pretty ordinary other than the whole changing into a wolf thing.

The team was back to training, and each day they spent time hunting Jason, the full shifter who got away. So far, they hadn't found him, but they weren't giving up, and if Jason was ever stupid enough to come back into our territory, they'd catch him.

They'd also added Tommy and Luken to their ranks, and as for the head enforcer, we'd let the guys vote. Surprisingly, they'd voted Landon into the position. I'd expected it to be Beck, but I had to admit, Landon was doing a fan-freakin-tastic job at it so far. Since he'd taken over, the rest of the pack were warming up to them, talking to them. They no longer walked in the other direction when they saw an enforcer coming.

It was nice. A nice and much-needed change.

Somehow I hadn't expected things to just go on. But I guessed that was how life worked. You went on. You moved forward. And ultimately, you became stronger for it.

I reached Aidan's office, and I inched open the door, trying to keep quiet. The last thing I wanted to do was wake the boys again before Mom got here to pick them up. They were both sprawled out on the couch, breathing evenly, and Cody had a thumb stuck in his mouth. It was probably evil of us to let them sleep now. They'd be crazy hyper when they woke up, but secretly, I thought Mom liked it that way.

Mom hadn't asked about Dad yet. She didn't question us on what happened or ask where the werecougars were. But I thought she probably already knew. Actually, I was sure she'd figured it out the moment we brought the kids home with us.

Aidan glanced up from his computer and smiled. It was a relaxed, contented smile, and seeing it made my entire body warm. I'd never seen him so content, so happy, and I loved it. Simply loved it.

I went straight to his desk, pulled out the chair he was sitting on, and plopped down on his lap, exhausted.

"Where's Tara?" he whispered, wrapping his arms around my waist, and pressing a light kiss onto my neck, just below my ear.

"Modeling her new clothes for Dom," I whispered back. "He's helping her pick what to wear for her first day at school on Monday."

Aidan chuckled and shook his head. "You're a very mean girl, Jade Shaw."

"No, I'm not." I cut him a look. "He likes it, I swear. He used to do it with Mac and me all the time." I snuggled into him, resting my head on his shoulder. "Anything interesting happen while we were gone?"

"Maybe," he said with a mischievous edge to his voice. I wiggled on his lap and looked up at him, arching a brow, and he chuckled. "I thought Mac was the gossiper."

"Spill it, buddy," I said in the sternest voice I could manage, which really wasn't that stern since I was still whispering. "I mean it. Tell me, or you'll be sleeping here tonight."

He made a face that clearly told me he knew that was

an empty threat, and he leaned into me and kissed me in that place just behind my ear, that place that always made me shiver.

"I might have walked in on Erika and Craig in the gym changing room this afternoon," he said.

"And what were they doing in the gym changing room, Aidan?" I asked, trying not to let his kisses distract me.

It wasn't working.

He continued to feather those light lip touches down my neck, and as he did, I felt as if I were falling, falling into that wonderful, warm place that I only ever found within his arms.

"I think you can figure that out," he whispered.

No kidding, I thought. I had a pretty good idea. Erika had been pretty relentless in her pursuit for his attention over the last week, and I knew it was only a matter of time before Craig stopped pretending he didn't care.

The door opened, and Mom breezed through. I jumped, and heat rushed to my cheeks. Aidan dislodged his lips from my neck but chuckled as I tried to wiggle off his lap, and he tightened his arms around my waist. I gave him a *look*, he smirked and gave me a *look*, and I rolled my eyes, and then I settled back against him.

Mom glanced at the boys, smiled, and then turned a scowl on us. "You let them sleep?" she asked. I thought she was trying for annoyance but didn't quite hit the mark. "Really, Aidan, it's too late for a nap. They'll be up all night now."

"You love it," he said, laughing. The boys began to stir, yawning loudly, and he laughed again.

"You're right," she muttered. "I do." She crossed over to the couch and smiled down at them. "Who's ready for some pizza?"

And there it was. The magic word.

The boys sprang to life, jumping off the couch, shouting, "Me," and ran for the door.

Mom laughed and waved a quick goodbye before chasing after them and telling them to go find their sister, which immediately led to both boys screaming out for Tara because that was, of course, easier than actually looking for her.

I sighed and shook my head, but I was smiling, a big, wide smile. I hadn't really expected it, at least not so soon, but we were okay. Mom, the kids, the pack ... We were really okay.

Aidan gave me a quick kiss as he leaned around me and started saving his work and shutting down the computer. "You ready to go home?" he asked. "The house should be ready for us by now."

I pulled his arms back around me when the computer shut down. His arms were always solid and safe and warm, and having them around me was like being wrapped up in comfort. "Yeah," I said. "I can't wait to see it."

I leaned back into him with a sigh, and his chest vibrated against my back as he chuckled. He rested his chin on my shoulder and whispered, "You know you're going to have to stand up if we're going home, right?"

I nodded. "I know." But I turned in his arms and kissed him, a sweet blend of heat and softness. I loved this. Bubbles of joy spread through me as his lips played with mine. I loved him. It had been a rough couple of months since he'd moved to town, and we'd both stumbled and fell and even crashed a few times, but it was worth it. The fight, the heartache, all of it was worth it to be here at this moment, feeling those bubbles tingle throughout my body.

When the kiss finally ended, we both dragged in a

strained breath, and he seemed to have trouble letting me go. His eyes, flecked with gold, searched my rosy cheeks. "You know," he said, cupping my face in his big warm hands, "I'm very lucky you love me."

"Yes. Yes, you are," I said, fixing my face in my most serious expression, which totally failed because my body was shaking with silent laughter as my happy bubbles began to burst and fill me with a giggly kind of bliss. "And I guess I'm pretty lucky you love me, too."

And then, as my laughter quieted and we got to our feet, I wondered what the future might hold for Aidan and me and our pack. I was pretty sure it wouldn't always be easy, but with his arm around my shoulder, holding me close to his side as we walked to the car, I felt completely at home, and that was more than enough for me.

Note from the Author

Thank you for reading *Deadly Pack*. If you enjoyed this book (or even if you didn't) please consider leaving a review on the site where you purchased it. Word-of-mouth is crucial for any author to succeed and your review, even if it's only a sentence or two, makes a huge difference in helping new readers make the decision to read my books. Many thanks for your support.

XOXO,
Ashley Stoyanoff

Acknowledgments

An enormous thank you goes to my family and friends. Thank you for your unwavering support and encouragement. I'm truly grateful to have you all in my life, and I love you all.

To my husband, Jordan, thank you for having so much patience and understanding, especially when I ignored you for days while working on *Deadly Pack*. You are the best!

And to my editor, Kathryn, I couldn't have finished this book without you. Thank you for being an invaluable member of my team.

Last, but not least, a huge thank you to all of my fabulous readers. You guys rock!

About the Author

Romance author Ashley Stoyanoff is the recipient of two Royal Dragonfly Book Awards for young adult and newbie fiction. Her first book, *The Soul's Mark: FOUND*, came out in 2012. Her other passions include reading and shopping for the latest fashions. Learn more about Ashley and her work at ashleystoyanoff.com.

Further Reading: Going Rogue

Did you love *Deadly Pack?* Then you should read *Going Rogue* by Ashley Stoyanoff!

We all die. Some of us sooner than later.

Alexa Cross never thought her existence would revolve around death. In life, as a nurse, she helped save people. But life has a funny way of throwing the unexpected because, in the afterlife, she spends her time watching people die and collecting their souls. As much as she wants to stop the deaths, she knows death is inevitable, and it cannot be stopped.

However, when a serial killer decides to take up shop in her district, Alexa can't sit back and do nothing. No one should die like that, and she's determined to alter Death's timeline. But, to do that, she needs to embrace who she is now and break some rules. It's the only chance she has of stopping the person responsible for the vicious murders.